A DIVIDED UNIVERSE

A Divided Universe

Vernon L. Anley

RESOURCE *Publications* • Eugene, Oregon

Resource Publications
A division of Wipf and Stock Publishers
199 W 8th Ave, Suite 3
Eugene, OR 97401

A Divided Universe
By Anley, Vernon L.
Copyright © 2014 by Anley, Vernon L. All rights reserved.
Softcover ISBN-13: 979-8-3852-3323-6
Hardcover ISBN-13: 979-8-3852-3324-3
eBook ISBN-13: 979-8-3852-3325-0
Publication date 9/16/2024
Previously published by Mirador Publishing, 2014

This edition is a scanned facsimile of the original edition published in 2014.

By the same author

A CARNIVAL OF LIES
AN UNHOLY LOVE
THE LAST SONG AND OTHER POEMS

INTRODUCTION

Because science cannot discover God among the galactic systems, religious skeptics assume that God does not exist, or at best is an 'illusion' or invention of the mind. While we argue that religion is a rational enterprise, having its starting point in a reality which is independent of us, this book seeks to establish a common ground on which men might meet, and enter into a new and higher collaboration in the pursuit of truth. To this end I have tried to elucidate briefly the sorts of considerations which are relevant to forming a view of life based on the existence of God and the activities of nature described by science.

To those who believe that we are mind, and the transcendence of the immanent God, our task is huge. We must create and live an ethics that optimizes human life and moves to the spiritual. To do this we must use our science, our knowledge of the mind of the immanent God. I am reminded of the words of the Talmudist: *'It is not up to you to finish the task: neither are you free to cease from trying.'*

Harold Morowitz

To someone who could grasp the Universe from a unified standpoint the entire creation would appear as a unique truth and necessity.
J.D'Alembert

When it is said that '*God is the Maker of heaven and earth and of all things visible and invisible*', the language is clearly symbolic. The category of creation itself is not mythical, but the imagery in which it is expressed is mythical in origin, but there is little doubt as to what is being said. It tells us, implicitly, something of crucial significance for the life and spirit of man. It tells us that the meaning and value of things cannot be separated from their origin, and that their source determines their ultimate nature and end. But today the imagery of creation points away from God to a more mundane reality: the cataclysmic explosion which we call the Big Bang.

Fifteen billion years ago an unimaginable eruption of energy broke through the nothingness of non-being and created space and time. Although the core ideas of the Big Bang (the expansion, the early hot state, the formation of helium, the formation of galaxies, etc.) are generally accepted, its cause is a mystery. Precisely because it is 'mystery', a term not acceptable to science, creation by *fiat* is rejected, and when answers are given, they are shaped by mathematical laws (which themselves are a mystery).

Among the scientists who maintain that there must be a 'scientific' explanation for the origin of the universe is Paul Atkins, Professor of Chemistry at Oxford University. Because Atkins believes that God is an 'epiphenomena of the brain' he says that only science can yield the true 'facts' about the universe and that it is foolish to look elsewhere for answers. In his book '*On Being*' (an extraordinary title for an atheist, since the notion of 'being' presupposes the possibility of transcendent knowledge), Atkins writes:

'I consider that there is nothing that it (science) cannot illuminate. Because the scientific method has not yet encountered a barrier, except the one asserted to exist by those fearful of its illumination, my optimism leads me to suppose that the reach of its beams is boundless and in particular that it can replace the myths that surround all the great questions of being.' Atkins then proceeds to answer, as best he can, the 'great questions of being.'

First among the 'great questions' answered by Atkins is the origin of the universe. Since Atkins' intention is to show 'that everything, including *Nothing,* is within science's reach,' he gives us his own unlikely account of creation - but admits, that when the correct answer is found 'it will be unrecognizably different from what I am about to describe.' Because the 'time' preceding the cosmological era or Big Bang is hidden, Atkins is forced to indulge in 'vacuous musing' to explain creation. Although conceding that his speculations are 'nonsense,' and they certainly read this way, he would have us believe that such ideas demonstrate that 'it is possible to think constructively about even the most apparent overwhelming problems and thereby undermine the view that our inception must have been an act of God.' In other words, no matter how ridiculous the idea, the fact that one can think such thoughts, eliminates the need for a creator.

It seems that man at each period of his history cherishes the delusion of the finality of his knowledge. At the present time scientists like Atkins are the leading dogmatists, denying that there is a dimension to human experience that takes man beyond the mere 'matter-of-fact.' All knowing must yield to observation and experiment. But it is precisely because science aims to explain the workings of the natural world through empirically testable theories that it cannot include knowledge of God. God is not a datum whose nature can be settled by looking up a handbook or by appealing to a set of experiments. Since one's awareness of God is never the result of an answer to the question of creation, atheists are wide of the mark by asking how God 'did this' or 'did that' – as if by such questions they hope to undermine belief in a creator.

Explanations of the origin of the universe which rely solely on the behavior of electrons or other elementary particles (string theory, wave function, etc.) leave man without a meaning or a purpose. We, actors in the drama of human living, are but stage-hands. The setting is magnificent, the lighting superb, the costumes gorgeous, but there is no play. If there is no 'end game' other than extinction, whatever meaning one derives from existence is fragmentary and short lived. Atkins tells us that science 'finds not the slightest hint of purpose in any event that it has examined.' Of course this is not quite true. The universe reveals an order, a design, and intelligibility that point in the direction of purpose, even if that purpose cannot be determined by science. But it is one thing to say that science cannot answer questions of ultimate purpose and quite another to dismiss purpose as an illusion. It is clearly beyond Atkins to imagine, let alone conceive, that this seething universe of mass and energy, of chemical processes, of endlessly varied plant and animal life, of human intelligence and love, should be the product of anything but a ball of flaming gas and the mindless forces of nature. For Atkins it is enough that he can appreciate the grandeur of the heavens 'just hanging there, wholly without purpose.'

More curious is the belief, which Atkins shares with many others, that the merging of science and religion is impossible because they are based on incompatible methodologies. Evolution is natural science, rigidly deterministic and reductionist, allowing no freedom and creativity; whereas religion is concerned with the meaning and value which informs human living and the freedom and creativity that is at its center. But this is not a matter of methodology, although there are differences in the principles and procedures of inquiry, but the failure to see that a dialogue between science and religion is both possible and necessary.

Atkins' refusal to consider an explanation for anything that cannot be answered in terms of 'normal science' suggests that he has had very little intercourse with people engaged in other disciplines. 'Something is' according to Atkins, because it *just happens to be*'. All the objects and laws in our sensible universe are only to be known as 'matters of fact'. But 'matters of fact' which cannot be explained are without any intrinsic reality - and so the alleged 'matter' would prove to be nothing. Since there is no technique or method of obtaining from physics or chemistry or biology or any other science an answer to the question, 'Why is there something and not nothing?' one must sooner or later be led to conceive a first cause, or condemn all human knowledge to mere matters of fact without explanation.

Atkins avoids this conundrum by saying that the task of science 'is to show something can come from nothing without intervention' (that is, without any statement that would make the existence of something comprehensible). According to this way of thinking, the universe, including life and mind, has 'come' from nothing and will end in nothing. He asks us to visualize a 'pre-space' or quantum vacuum from which our universe emerged without apparent reason (a 'cosmic blunder'). Even if one could imagine such a happening, one cannot conceive how the universe emerged from this pre-space without prior conditions - since it is these prior conditions that created the material for the universe in the first place. Atkins hides these 'prior conditions' (which if admitted would return us to the real world of 'something' and not 'nothing') behind the 'laws of nature.' Thus the 'laws of nature' are the invisible creator that hides within itself the prior conditions for the world's creation. But what makes them laws? And why are they necessary? The universe and humanity—our origin and existence—depend on these laws. But where do the laws come from? One of Einstein's most hackneyed sayings is, 'The most incomprehensible thing about the universe is that it is comprehensible.' What Einstein meant is that the laws of nature seem to apply not just here on earth, but everywhere in the universe. Atkins, on the other hand, argues that the laws of nature do not represent reality.

'My view is that a scientific law is just a summary of observation. So it's a summary of behaviour.' In other words, the laws of nature are human inventions which impose artificial constructs on reality. Of course if this were the case, they would not be necessary, and we would not be here.

Because science abjures mystery, when cosmologists look behind the Big Bang, they conjure explanations for what is inexplicable using theoretical models derived from computerized simulations. It has been suggested, for example, that the universe 'recycles' itself eternally from the detritus of former worlds. Even if it were possible for a collapsing universe to bounce back to a new expansion, and so on ad infinitum, it would still leave the question of its beginning unanswered. One can avoid this problem, as Atkins does, by saying that universe was 'born out' of nothing. But it is an axiomatic truth that if nothing exists, then 'nothing' will be, for nothing is simply nothing.

The ultimate fall back position for the atheist is to say, as Bertrand Russell did, that 'the universe is just there', eternal and uncreated. While one can envisage a static universe being 'just there', it is almost impossible to imagine a dynamic universe, where life appears driven by an evolutionary current towards ever increasing consciousness, appearing ready-made out of nowhere. This unlikely scenario need not detain us. All observational evidence suggests that our universe is expanding, so it must have had a beginning sometime in the past.

So far from accounting for existence, all cosmological theories raise the question of creation. For something to be entirely self-sufficient it must be at the very least be eternal, uncaused, and indestructible. But since the universe lacks these attributes, it must owe its origin to something that exists independently of space and time, that is not contingent, but is eternal and self-existent. Moreover, since mind is not only one of the facts of the world, but is the ruling principle of existence itself; creation can only be explained by a cause that is essentially spiritual. The only way to avoid this conclusion is to deny that anything that exists must have a reason for its existence, which is absurd.

The radical defect in all theories that deny a transcendent creator is that they fail to explain the origin of things, or why they exist at all. Science tells us that our earth is what it is because it was once part of the nebula, and that mankind is an insignificant accident lost in the immensity of the cosmos. This world view was eloquently stated by the physicist Steven Weinberg in his popular book on cosmology, *The First Three Minutes*:

'It is almost irresistible for humans to believe that we

have some special relation to the universe, that human life is not just a more-or-less farcical outcome of a chain of accidents reaching back to the first three minutes of the universe's existence, but that we were somehow built in from the beginning... It is very hard to realize that the entire earth is just a tiny part of an overwhelmingly hostile universe. It is even harder to realize that this present universe has evolved from an unspeakably unfamiliar early condition, and faces a future extinction of endless cold or intolerable heat. The more the universe seems comprehensible, the more it also seems pointless.'

On the face of it, Weinberg's pessimism seems justified, although his scenario of life may not be quite so short term as he envisages. Long before the end we will have taken steps to colonize the universe. Probes will have been sent on exploratory missions to far flung galaxies to determine if stellar systems exist capable of supporting life. Since such sympathetic environments are likely to be many hundreds, if not thousands of light years distant, it will be necessary, if such locations are found, for probes, programmed to synthesize fertilized human egg-cells, to deliver our nascent offspring to their new home. These offspring could be raised to adulthood by robots, and in due course develop their own civilizations. Olaf Stapledon, whose influence on the development of science fiction ideas is probably second only to that of H.G. Wells, suggested that we may be able to disseminate the seeds of a new humanity among the stars through the use of human spores. By tethering immense quantities of such spores to minute electro-magnetic 'wave systems', individually capable of sailing on solar winds to the most distant reaches of the galaxy, they could find a suitable environment and embark upon biological evolution as occurred on earth many millions of years ago.

As intriguing as such ideas are, escape into other worlds, whether in far flung galaxies, or in self–sustaining human colonies in space, is not so much a new beginning as the beginning of the end. Stellar births are still occurring, but due to the exhaustion of hydrogen and the dissipation of the galaxies, in 10^{12} years star formation will cease and bring to an end the energy necessary for life. Even if alternative forms of energy become available, positron decay will eventually exhaust the resources of the universe leaving a featureless, infinitely large void. Although no organic life form can survive in a universe as the final singularity is approached, other forms of intelligent beings (self-replicating machines with intelligence comparable to a human level) may continue until the end of space-time. These machines may be our ultimate heirs. Although it may be possible for such robots to survive many billions of years beyond the span of all carbon-based life forms, there is little joy in thinking that the goal of human endeavour are robots that will ultimately self destruct as the universe approaches its end. In any event, a time will come when the universe will have decayed into a state of featureless equilibrium. All the wreckage of the galaxies will have dissolved into an electron-positron plasma at which time neither black holes, nor stars, nor planets, nor any other material or tangible substance remains.

In a mechanistically driven universe life and death are subject to the laws that will ultimately subdue all life and bring the universe to an end. A physically dominant universe offers nothing but death. This is the fate of all matter, including ourselves, if we are but physical objects. The full weight of this depressing scenario was etched in words by Bertrand Russell:

'That man is the product of causes that had no prevision of the end they were achieving; that his origin, his growth, his hopes and fears, his love and his beliefs, are but the outcome of accidental collocation of atoms; that no fire, no heroism, no intensity of thought and feeling, can preserve individual life beyond the grave; that all the labours of the ages, all the devotion, all the inspiration, all the noonday brightness of human genius, are destined to extinction in the vast death of the solar system, and that the whole temple of man's achievement must inevitably be buried beneath the debris of a universe in ruins...'

If we are to believe Russell, we have no choice but to meet the absolutely irrevocable ordinance of death without hope.

It is difficult to imagine that anyone could survey the entire story of matter, life, and mind, from star dust to human evolution, without an overwhelming impression that the universe is driven by meaning and purpose. Both Weinberg and Russell opt for cosmic pessimism, but their writings reveal that they can no more evade the search for meaning than we ourselves can. In the closing remarks of his book, Weinberg says 'The effort to understand the universe is one of the very few things that lifts human life a little above the level of farce and gives it some of the grace of tragedy.' Weinberg finds meaning in science (one might almost say that it becomes his religion), whereas Russell, towards the end of his life, admitted that 'the real cause of a thing's being what it is, is to be sought not in the past but rather in the future.' In the last resort we can only experience life as meaningful if we are prepared to deny that the universe is not static but dynamic, not undirected, but directed by an immanent intelligibility towards a purposeful future.

When science won its battle with the Church for the freedom to entertain its own hypothesis, it in turn became the principle repository of the ideas that particular forms of knowledge could either be absolute truths or at least could approach absolute truths. While scientists like Atkins and Dawkins still cling to the hope that science will bring them to some notion of absolute truth, many others have accepted the need for change in their basic concepts. The most radical, one might almost say mystical view on the nature of the universe, was proposed by Teilhard de Chardin, the French philosopher and Jesuit priest who trained as a paleontologist and geologist.

Teilhard saw that the unity and permanence that science seeks is found only in the 'eternal mind' in whose consciousness all things have their being. Thus the starting point of creation was not undifferentiated matter, but Spirit. He saw that if the sequence of events involved in the evolutionary development of the universe relied solely on the physical properties of matter it left no place for man. Spirit saves and ennobles matter, carrying it forward and sustaining it constantly in its ascent towards consciousness. The material world was created by spirit, driven by spirit, and would, when biological genesis reaches the full term of its potential, shed its material skin and reunite with its source: '... and God may be all in all' (1 Cor. 15:28).

For Teilhard there was no conflict between religion and science any more than there is between spirit and matter, for these have been artificially separated. The conflict needs to be resolved, not in elimination, nor duality, but in synthesis – in the mutual reinforcement of these two still opposed disciplines. It is the claim of this book that too many scientists have been content to accept the universe on the basis of facts derived from observation, while treating intuitions of God as unnecessary or incidental. If we begin with mindless and valueless data there is no place for intelligence and morality as noted by Teilhard. Although science sees space-time as the all-pervasive matrix of all that is, and abjures the notion of a transcendent reality, we must seek an alternative approach which favors the subtle orderings of spirit rather than mathematical determinism to account for the emergence of consciousness and spirit in man.

2

*Science cannot solve the ultimate mystery of Nature.
And it is because in the last analysis we ourselves are
part of the mystery we are trying to solve.*
M. Plank

Atkins is not alone in rejecting a spiritual
foundation for material existence. Richard Dawkins is
another scientist who believes that science unaided by
religion provides the best interpretation of the
universe. Given man's evolutionary potential, one
might think that a biologist would be more interested
in the possibilities of man's future than to labor to
prove the folly of religion. Yet Dawkins seems more
keen to denounce religious experience ('I am utterly
fed up with the respect we have been brainwashed into
bestowing upon religion') than seeking new insights
into the nature of being.

Although there is no reason why religion and science
should experience any conflict, there have always been
those (at least since Plato's time) who refuse to consider
that while science offers the factual truth about nature,
such facts do not explain the origin of things. In 'The
Sophist' Plato is bemused by the fact that men of

apparent common sense rely wholly on mechanist assumptions for their understanding of reality:

STRANGER – One side drags down everything from heaven and the unseen to the earth, rudely grasping rocks and trees in their hands. For they get their grip on all such things and they maintain that that alone exists which can be handled and touched. They define body and existence as the same thing, and if anyone says that one of the other things which does not have a body exists they completely despise him and are unwilling to listen to another word.

THEAETETUS – Terrible men they are of whom you speak. I myself have met with a lot of them in my time.

Dawkins like the 'terrible men' that Plato speaks of, believes that 'Human beings are simply machines for propagating DNA, and the propagation of DNA is a self-sustaining process. It is every living object's sole reason for living' (*The Selfish Gene*). This rigidly deterministic approach, which allows no freedom or creativity, views living organisms as vehicles at the mercy of the blind forces of selection through which genes relentlessly propagate themselves. 'We are survival machines – robot vehicles blindly programmed to preserve the selfish molecule known as genes.' Because of this Dawkins can declare that 'The universe we observe has precisely the properties we should expect if there is, at bottom, no design, no purpose, no evil, and no good, nothing but blind pitiless indifference.' In short, the ultimate meaning of life is that there is no meaning.

This conclusion is inevitable if life, as Dawkins assumes, is a fortuitous accident. Although as an explanation for the origin of life it is difficult to imagine even at the most cosmic level of chance probabilities. Once life appears it ensures its survival by propagating the genetic material necessary for evolution. Dawkins tells us that our daily lives are nothing but an incubator for the propagation of this hereditary material (DNA). We are locked in a world of mechanical necessity, at the mercy of the 'Selfish Gene.' But among language-using humans the world of daily life is never all there is, and the other realities that culture gives rise to cannot fail but overlap the everyday world whose relentless utilitarianism can never be absolute.

In 1837, in the first of many notebooks he was going to keep on the 'species problem,' Darwin stressed the continuity of life and how all living things are descended from a single ancestor. Why this process occurred remains a riddle, as is the occurrence of life itself. What Darwin said in his *Origin of Species* is still true. 'The laws governing inheritance are for the most part unknown.' One may rejoice in one's biological uniqueness and biological antiquity with all other forms

17

of life, but it is plain that we are not wholly engaged with our environment and self preservation. Human desires are not simply the biological impulses of hunger for eating and of sex for mating. Indeed, man is an animal for whom mere animality is indecent. If the matter-of-fact world were the paramount reality (as prescribed by gene theory) we would be locked in a world of dreadful immanence – for according to standard evolutionary theory, the primary function of both intelligence and emotion is to enable us to survive and reproduce. In fact one cannot live in the world of 'daily life' all the time. It is too 'matter of fact', too utilitarian: it is without promise or purpose. It must be punctuated with periods that are more inherently gratifying, with activities that are not means to an end. Without the capacity for transcendence, man would, in the words of French biologist, Jacques Monod, 'live on the boundary of an alien world; a world that is deaf to his music, and is indifferent to his hopes as it is to his sufferings and crimes.'

As it happens most evolutionary biologists believe that it is the organism that evolves, and not just the genes. Because the organism participates in its own evolution, it is not genetically controlled. If this is the case the argument that the unit of biological selection is the gene and that the organism is a 'throwaway survival machine' (Dawkins) is mistaken. Because the organism can learn, and learning can change the organism's environment (and thus the survival chances of its offspring), it is the organism – and not the gene, that is the central unit of evolution. When it comes to the point, the known facts of biology can be summed up in the statement that there is deep within life itself a power of variation and a persistent tendency to perfect itself.

Although Dawkins puts great store by Darwin, and quotes freely from 'The Origin of Species' to support his theories, he ignores the fact that Darwin became more agnostic as he grew older: 'It is impossible to conceive this immense and wonderful universe, including man... as the result of blind chance or necessity. When thus reflecting I feel compelled to look to a First Cause having an intelligent mind in some degree analogous to that of man and I deserve to be called a theist. I am inclined to look at everything as resulting from designed laws, and that these ultimately may be set by rational and transcendent power legitimately called God.'

Dawkins breaks with Darwin and insists that human intelligence can be explained in material terms, and that the appearance of 'designed laws' is illusory since evolution can be explained by chance and necessity (although the entire idea of 'chance' and 'randomness' is rejected by many evolutionists as cause in biology, at least in phenomena above the quantum level). Similarly he refutes Paley's argument that the discovery of a watch in a field would lead one to assume the existence of a designer by showing how design arose through natural selection. But Dawkins misses the point. The point is not how, when or where the watch was designed but the fact that it is designed. Dawkins confuses the mechanism by which evolution works with assumptions about its origin and cause.

In the drama of human living it is clear that man is not, as science would have him believe, just another animal, a little more advanced than most perhaps, but one of the brutes none the less. Furthermore since man is the product of a blind evolutionary process, there is no reason for supposing that he has any meaningful future in store for him. It would be more realistic to conclude that he will eventually disappear into the darkness from which he emerged.

The believer feels the absurdity of this even more deeply. Science has led us to see death as the definite ending of a human being; and while it has relieved us of the notion that 'having to die' is due to an original primeval fall, it does nothing to lessen the attack death makes on our right to exist by removing us completely and inexorably from ourselves and those we leave behind. Eternity does not belong to mankind, but we cannot escape the idea of it. Are we written off along with our corporality at death as atheists suppose, or is there, as our deepest instinct would have us believe, an imperishable essence in the human person that bypasses death?

Even if one denies the claims made for man's creation in Genesis, his appearance marks a completely new dimension in the development of life forms. Intelligence and rational consciousness are not subject to physical laws, nor are they part of the material world that makes up the multiplicity of matter. The attainment of self-consciousness, which constitutes true intelligence, is the prerogative of man alone and represents a radical advance on all preceding forms of life. Animals know; but it is equally certain that *they cannot know what they know.* Hence a whole domain of reality is closed to them, a domain in which we for our part can move freely. Reflective consciousness makes us not merely different from our closest relatives in the animal kingdom, but wholly other. It is a difference not merely of degree but of kind: a change of nature, resulting from a change of state.

When we consider the nature of human intelligence, it becomes clear that we are not dealing simply with neural processes and patterns. We are, in fact, compelled to make a distinction between the material and what Plato called the *'nous'* or spirit. Quite clearly man is both material and spiritual; he is material in as much as he is a biological organism, but he is also spiritual by reason of his intelligence (that neither is constituted nor is conditioned intrinsically by his physical and chemical properties). But man is not just an assemblage of parts. He is intelligibly one, and this unity has its ground in the 'I' that he knows to be himself.

Crucial for our understanding of man is whether this 'I' is material or spiritual. As long as the alternatives are merely described, it is possible to straddle the issue: for man's central form seems to be the point of transition from the material to the spiritual. Man's sensitive experience (touch, taste, smell, etc.) is determined by his physical properties; but it is no less a fact that inquiry and insight, understanding and reflection, are independent of his material body. A solution seems to result from a simple principle, namely, that were man's central form material, it could not be intelligent and so could not be the center and ground of his inquiry and insight, reflection and judgment. Inversely, if man's form were spiritual, it could be the ground and center of his material being; for the spiritual is comprehensive; what can embrace the whole universe through knowledge can provide the center and ground of unity in the material properties of a single man. If the answer is accepted, it raises the intriguing question whether the breakdown of his organic and sensitive living is necessarily the end of his personal existence. *'If a man die, shall he live again?'* asked Job. His friends do not answer him directly, but point out that mere bodily existence does not constitute life. Man exists and functions physically. Death is a witness to the breakdown of his organic body. But because his central form is spiritual, he could, absolutely speaking, be separated from his material being without losing his identity. Since the spiritual is imperishable, death need not mean the surrender of the last vestiges of his individuality and separate existence. An empirical conjunction is not a metaphysical necessity. Presumably Plato had a similar idea in mind when he has Crito ask Socrates, 'In what way shall we bury you?' Socrates answers, 'In any way you like, but first you must catch *me*, the real me. Be of good cheer, my dear Crito, and say that you are burying my body only, and do with *that* whatever is usual and what you think best.'

All religions presume that God establishes a relationship of mutual immanence with the human soul, and therefore ensures its survival. In the Bhagavad-Gītā which, among the classical Hindu scriptures, claims to be a direct revelation from God, the stages of death are clearly defined. First there is the integration of the personality into the immortal ground, implied in the phrase 'to become Brahman'. Then, after becoming Brahman, the soul 'rejoices' in the bliss of God's love: this means that in eternity personal relationships, at least as between the soul and God, remain. Life is affirmed as the permanent principle of existence in which the death of the individual is no more than the transformation of one mode of life into another. In terms of our earthly existence, our lives are short-lived, and count for little when compared with the relatively permanent things around us. But if our lives are taken up into God's own existence , it is the world that passes away, and it is we who continue for ever.

The love of God in the context of pure spirituality which appears in the Upanishads reaches its peak in the New Testament. John's language in Revelations is highly pictorial, punctuated by voices and bursts of heavenly hymnody, especially when he himself experiences a mystical death and resurrection. 'Fear not, I am the first and the last, and the living one, I died, and behold I am alive for evermore.' Ecstatic words! But the best is yet to come. Life in the new Jerusalem is permanently incandescent. 'And the city had no need of the sun, neither of the moon, to shine in it: for the glory of God did lighten it.' And suffering is a thing of the past. 'God shall wipe away all tears from their eyes; and there shall be no more death, neither sorrow, nor crying, nor shall there be any more pain: for the former things have passed away.' John speaks of truths beyond human comprehension, of values beyond human estimation, of an alliance of love that, so to speak, brings man too close to God.

Although such formulations concerning the Divine life and its relation to the life of man transcend the possibility of human assertion and violate the mystery of the divine 'abyss', theologians point out that such descriptions, symbolic as they are, affirm the ultimate seriousness of life in the light of the eternal; for a world which is only external to God and not also internal to him, in the last consideration, is a divine play of no essential concern for God.

While the question, 'What next?' comes naturally to man, it cannot be answered. Death is the vanishing point of all experience. There is no beyond it. Paul, never hesitant to ascribe reality to that which can only be answered in terms of eschatological imagery, denies the nakedness of a merely spiritual existence after death and that we are 'preserved entire'. In Colossians and Ephesians the hymnic language is high-flown, suggesting exciting possibilities in the supernatural world. In Romans, death is the 'baptismal' separation of spirit from matter. Resurrection is not a day of assembly but the bestowal of a new form to our spirit (soma pneumatic): the spiritually transformed total personality of man. In some sense we are both ourselves and distinct from ourselves, a 'new creation'. This corresponds to the apparition stories about Jesus. All agree that he was 'experienced' in his total personality, including the bodily expression of his being: 'We have seen the Lord' and 'We know him now.'

Whether life is the movement of individuals out of

the earthly realm into the heavenly realm, we can be sure that our evolutionary potential has not been exhausted. Deceived by the slowness of movements that embrace the whole universe, we find it difficult to think of man still moving along his evolutionary trajectory. What changed our pre-human ancestors into human beings like ourselves was the acquisition of consciousness and will. These two spiritual faculties are man's distinguishing marks, and are the pointers to his further development. For the religious minded, the saints represent the growing point of human evolution. They proclaim, by their very existence, character and consciousness, that humanity can rise above its assumed limitations, that the tide of evolution is pushing forward to a new high level.

Darwinian's tell us that man in his temporal-historical existence is an animal and a mediocre biological success. As such he has neither purpose nor meaning other than as a function of a process he has little or no control over. A depressing picture that leaves the world unattended and man without hope. There is no greater contrast than this notion of man's being and miserable future, than Paul's proclamation that 'Whether we live, we live unto the Lord; and whether we die, we die unto the Lord. For in him we live, and move, and have our being' (Romans 14:8). Life is the historical realization of God's will, which of its very nature implies openness to the future and to new historical horizons. The atheist may deny it. The agnostic may urge that his investigation has been inconclusive. The contemporary humanist will refuse to allow the proposition to arise. But their negations presuppose the spark in our clod, our native orientation towards the divine.

3

If there are genuine laws which control the physical world, they are of a transcendental character.
Eddington

If life was a precarious adventure, and man nothing but a bundle of atoms, atheism would come naturally to man and religion would be the prerogative of the lunatic fringe. They would be ridiculed for believing in an illusory divine being that endows man with a spirit and a destiny not limited to the sensible world. But in reality it is the pragmatist who adheres to that which cannot be seen and is ultimately unknown. His world is not a concrete actuality, but an abstract idea. Modern physics has reduced the world of immediate experience to fields of energy. Photons, gravitons, and gluons and such like 'particles' are not observable phenomena. They are given as real since they fulfill the requirements of this or that theory, but have no discrete existence. Reality, as conceived by pragmatism, cannot be reduced to mere matters of fact. The ultimate structure of the universe is not known to science. Newton's mechanical conception as much as Einstein's is a conceptual model, abstract and partial.

Our scientific theories are only links in a long chain of progressive advances likely in time to be themselves replaced. They are temporary resting places in the search for truth and there is nothing absolute about them. Since the subject matter of science is abstractions from the real, it offers us a purely mechanical explanation for creation. Lifeless particles careered about for billions of years and in their interaction created myriads of nebula, of suns, our own solar system, and by some remarkable transformation, life itself. No principle outside the natural world is needed to account for the appearance of man. Man is looked upon as a psycho-chemical being, a biological unit of the human species. The dynamic-creative nature of man's personal and communal life – his spirit, is relegated to the non-rational corner of subjective emotion. Similarly, the idea of God, which has had an unbroken sway from the most primitive ages of human history, is given a psychological explanation. Freud insists that the history of religion is nothing else than a history of illusion. But if the object of belief were only imaginary, created in order to satisfy our needs, then the belief itself would in time wither away. No man can worship permanently what is untrue.

If one's only aid to knowledge was the telescope, it would seem that the universe does not have any definite purpose which it is attempting to realize. To be born, to live, to die and to begin all over again, until all things have disappeared as though nothing had even been accomplished, such is the process of the universe, such is its destiny. Lucretius (99BC- 55BC) who took refuge in the high indifference of atoms storming through the void, set the path for a 'naturalist' interpretation of existence by saying that life is guided by *fortuna*, 'chance' and not divine intervention. In line with the Roman philosopher and poet, Bertrand Russell said that any religion that has God at its centre will be replaced by a stoicism that accepts the universe as it is and expects nothing from it. There is an element of the sublime in this stoicism, which submits to necessity or chance: but it is difficult to maintain an attitude of noble despair in a meaningless universe. If the universe is a lifeless background of irresponsible energy against which the drama of human life is played, it is unlikely that life would ever have made a start. Loyalty to life requires us to believe that existence is purposeful. Unless there is something which at all costs must be, and is the source of the significance of everything that happens in time and space, life would be nothing but a meaningless episode on a twirling speck of cosmic rock. The setting may be magnificent, the lighting superb, but there is no play.

If we are to believe the American biologist E O Wilson, 'Scientific humanism is the only world view compatible with science's growing knowledge of the real world and laws of nature.' In common with all humanism, the scientific humanist believes that the only values that matter are human values, and denies that such values have a transcendent source. But if such values are simply 'incidents in the empirical growth of things,' or creations of the human mind, with no permanent underpinning in a transcendent moral ground, it is unlikely that they would count for much. Still, it is the argument that humans are merely physical bodies that undercuts the humanist ideal. If minds are wholly dependent on brains, and brains on biochemistry, and biochemistry on the meaningless flux of atoms, how does one account for rational consciousness? Matter is that which has mass and occupies space. But consciousness is neither constituted nor is it conditioned by the material residue. It is a spiritual reality, unfettered by our material body, which orientates us towards a universe of being.

There exists in man a faculty above and beyond the biological account books of pleasure and pain. Conscious living is itself a joy that shows itself in the untiring play of children, in the swing of a melody, in the joy of a sunlit morning. Such delight is not, perhaps, exclusively human, for kittens play and snakes are charmed. But neither is it merely biological. Rather, one is led to believe that man's sensitivity slips beyond the confines of genetic conditioning, and liberates consciousness from the drag of biological intent. As human intelligence develops more and more importance is attached to transcending himself, of ceasing to be an animal in a habitat, into a universe designated by meaning. It constitutes social systems, endows them with cultural significance, and reveals the direction and momentum of life.

The heroes of humanity, its Buddhas and Christs, its Platos and Paul, are all shaped after the same pattern of experience and understanding, differing from the ordinary man only in their heightened awareness of their identity with the spiritual source of the universe. They assert that the spiritual is the basis and background of our being, the universality that cannot be reduced to this or that formula. Among the religious teachers the Buddha is marked out as the one who admitted the reality of the spiritual experience and yet refused to interpret it as revelation of anything beyond itself. However since he proclaimed the ultimate salvation of all beings, on the basis of their common identify with Eternal Righteousness (dharma), one must presume that he had man's spirit in mind.

The consubstantiality of the spirit in man and God is the conviction of all spiritual wisdom. We belong to the real and the real is mirrored in us. The Upanishad says, *Tat tvam asi* (That art thou) and Jesus told his disciples 'I and my father are one.' It is not a peculiar relation between any one chosen individual and God, but an ultimate one binding every self to God. No one on earth has ever maintained a conscious spiritual connection with God throughout his life. Great saints are rare, and even they call themselves vessels of clay. The Jesus who declared that man must not resist evil and love one's enemy, was the same Jesus that cursed the fig tree and drove the tradesmen from the temple. To keep one's faith in the face of an uncomprehending and hostile world is not a light affair. If the goal is always distant it is not inhuman, for it corresponds to the dynamic structure of man's being, to the restlessness that is ours till we rest in God.

No one will be surprised that science, precisely because it is geared to knowledge of this world, cannot yield knowledge of God. Knowledge of God, then, is a singular case. It is not immediate knowledge: there is no data on the divine itself. It is not verifiable knowledge: there are no verifiable hypotheses or principles without data. What kind of knowledge, then, is it? Traditionally, it has been interpreted as intuitive, that is, a form of knowing spontaneously derived from or prompted by a natural tendency. If this is the case it would seem that one's` intuition of God precedes our knowledge of him and, indeed, may be the cause of our seeking to know him. Intuitive knowledge is an orientation to transcendent mystery, the bond uniting all men despite cultural differences. In moving from intellect to intuition we are not moving in the direction of reason, but are getting into the deepest rationality of which human nature is capable. When Plato tells us that 'that which imparts truth to the known and the power of knowing to the knower, is what I would have you term the Idea of the Good', he is asking us to recognize that the apprehension of the real is not a matter of logical knowledge, but is prior to the distinction of subject and object, of truth and error, which arise at the reflective level. Pascal's saying that the heart has its reasons which reason does not know is well known. It is not argument, nor the so-called proofs of God's existence that bring one to God, but the incontrovertible experience of an intensely personal, reciprocal relationship between ourselves and that which holds the power of life in its hands.

4

Prior to an individual's encounter with the love of God at a particular time in history, however, there has to be another, more fundamental and archetypal encounter, which belongs to the conditions of possibility of the appearance of divine love to man.
Hans Urs von Balthasar

Man has a religious awareness which is the source of his religious experience: an *imago Dei*, an original intuition which gives meaning to the whole of human life in the world and in society. For the religious-minded inquirer religion is the highest form of human activity. It is a mode of consciousness which its distinct from the perceptual, imaginative or intellectual, and carries with it self-evidence and completeness. It offers Man the greatest opportunity of gaining insight into reality, and of entering into contact with it, that is open to him in this life. For those who hold this view, the skeptic's contention that religion is an illusion robs life of its meaning and purpose. Conversely, for the skeptic, a rational understanding of reality is made impossible by the believer's contention that the essence of reality is a spiritual presence which, from the rationalist's point of view, is imaginary, because it can only be vouched for by personal experience and cannot be verified by observation. But while rational thought can discover an intelligible system of regular and therefore predictable uniformities and recurrences, spiritual truths are not of this kind, and are, by definition, unverifiable. In short, the answers to the questions that matter most to us can only be found in a religious experience by which one enters into a subject-to-subject relation with God. It is the reason of the heart that reason does not know.

Religion has had a bad press. The wars of religion are legion, and much of the killing and carnage reported almost daily is laid at the feet of religion. But it is not just the follies and crimes committed in the name of the various religions that lead one to conclude that none of them can either be good or true, nor is it the fact that all religions, to a greater or lesser extent, affront reason, but rather the fact that the paradoxes from which they start are so distressingly at variance with one another. Their only common ground is to provide release: but there is absolutely no agreement at all as to what it is that man must be released from.

It is a sad fact that religion which would bring us closer to God and to man, can bring hostility against God, man, and even one's self. This disjunction exposes religion to all kinds of new risks, such as the tendency to retreat into the limited sphere of privacy where it still seems to have a place; or to reduce religion to ethics, or simply to long nostalgically for the old view of the church in which religion was the all embracing and integrating factor of society. Although the institutional aspects of religions have been opened up to serious questioning, not a single sociological analysis has shown that the religious and spiritual dimensions of human life have ceased to engage people.

Given the ineffectual response to violence which we see daily, it is only too clear that practical solutions, based on common sense, merely shift conflict and, at best, produce a temporary suppression of hostility. Such short term fixes must be replaced by a solution that respects the individuality and kinships of all men. One might expect that anthropology, since it studies humanity in all its aspects, would welcome religion as answer to the problem of evil: but on the contrary, it takes religion to be a 'secular phenomena' with little constructive significance for humanity. Its investigators have determined that man's religious rituals are the substance of religion itself. Fitzroy Sommerset (a former President of the Royal Anthropological Institute) put it this way: 'Rituals make up religion. For the religious, or the vast majority of them, they are not merely a part of religion, but religion itself.' Most religious people, on the contrary, would say that Sommerset could not see the wood for the trees. While not denying the importance of ritual in religion, they would argue that the essence of religion lies not in the ritual act itself, but to that which it points. Without the capacity for symbolic transcendence, for seeing the realm of daily life in terms of a realm beyond it, without the capacity for 'beyonding,' one would be trapped in a world of dreadful immanence. For the world of daily life seen solely as a world of rational response to anxiety and need is a world of mechanical necessity, not radical autonomy. It is through pointing to other realities that religion, through ritual, breaks the dreadful fatalities of this world of appearances.

Emile Durkheim, considered by many to be the father of sociology, noted that all known religious beliefs divide the world into two domains, the sacred and the profane. He noted further that man's attitude towards sacred things was essentially the same as the social and moral deference that he felt for his community. Durkheim's life's work culminated in *Les Formes élémentaires de la vie religieuse* (The Elementary Forms of religious Life, 1912). Durkheim based his studies on the Arrernte people, an Australia aboriginal tribe living in the Northern Territory – without ever having been to Australia, without ever having seen an aboriginal, and without ever having witnessed one of their ceremonies.

Durkheim chose the Arrernte people because he thought that their beliefs were the most primordial and fundamental manifestation of religion, and thus the key to understanding the origin of religious experience. His research led him to conclude, since the aborigine was mistaken in believing that an animal or plant could induce a state of reverence (without considering that such 'objects' are metaphors for a genuine sensory experience) that the true object of veneration is society itself. 'Respect for the moral authority of a society is like the respect for a God, and while man believes that he owes all he has to the gods, he does in fact owe all he has to society.' Durkheim reached this conclusion from the fact that believers at different times and in different parts of the world have had widely diverging perceptions of reality – but experience the same religious awe. There is then a reality behind the articles of faith – and that reality is society! This reasoning led him to develop a theory which conceives the personification of supernatural beings to arise directly from the nature of society itself. Thus Monotheism arises from sovereign states; polytheism from societies where certain activities are clearly differentiated (fishing, hunting, etc); the worship of ancestral spirits in societies which have strong kinship organizations; and reincarnation when associated with Brahmanism. In other words, religion, and the revelation it bears witness to, is nothing but belief in an image formed after a particular model of society.

In spite of the many exceptions, there is a correspondence between sovereign groups and their religion. But classifications based on economic and political factors are one thing: it is quite another to conclude that the object of religious worship is society itself. On the contrary, rather than being the creation of a familial or social group, religion has made man spiritually independent of the social order in which he finds himself. It has given him the strength to stand against the norms and institutions of society as an independent moral power and, in the last resort to disobey its commands if he judges these to be in conflict with his conscience.

The facts of religious experience are universal, in space and time. They are found in different parts of the world and different periods in history, attesting to the persistent unity and aspiration of the human spirit. Neither society nor the great civilizations of the World have produced religion as a kind of cultural by-product – if anything, the reverse is true: religion is the foundation on which the great civilizations rest. Religions have been tempted or driven into serving as means to non-religious ends; but to take these episodes of their history as being their raison d'être is to misunderstand their mission.

The higher religions teach us that the infinite presents itself in various forms, but in one form or another it is always there as an essential part of the religious consciousness. St Paul tells us that 'the love of God is shed abroad in our hearts by the Holy Ghost which is given unto us' (Romans 5:5). Likewise, in the Koran, that God is nearer to us than our very heart beat. St. Augustine, that he is more inward than one's innermost being. The mysticism of ancient India, that man is one with Brahma, and St Thomas 'the inner instinct which urges and moves us to faith.' While God may be conceived rationally as the ground of the universe, those who know God personally as the 'Thou' they interiorly address, will tell you that they know God as a living reality in their lives. From this fact flows the ritual, rites, ceremonies, and traditions that the religiously minded express their beliefs both symbiotically and explicitly.

There exists, then, in man a capacity for love that, in its immediacy, regards not the ever passing shape of this world but the mysterious reality, immanent and transcendent, that we name God. Although deeply personal, this love is not so private as to be solitary. The Spirit is given to many and the many form a community. It acquires a history of its origins, its developments, its successes and failures. But an organized religion is not a conventicle of saints. It is like a net cast into the sea that catches all sorts of fish. Because Christians are not all saints, their weaknesses show up in their outward behavior and organizations. There is always a gap between the ideal and the real, between religion as it strives to be, and religion as it is in fact. But its mistakes and failures do not argue for religion's abolition, but for its reform.

5

Jesus cried out and said, 'Whoever believes in me does not believe in me, but in him who sent me.'
John: 12:44

It is an extraordinary irony that Christianity, the religion that claims to have irreducible evidence of God, casts the most doubt on his existence. For many people this is because of the New Testament's statements that Jesus stands beside God as a divine being with God's own attributes (in three instances John actually calls Jesus 'God'). With Jesus' makeover the New Testament breaks away from the Old Testament and enters upon the world of the Son. In the Old Testament life was not only given by Yahweh but its preservation was acknowledged as being dependent on God. Whereas it was precisely life's connection with God that was absolute, the reverse is true in the New Testament. By incarnating in the Son, God is reduced to 'the Father'. Like the sun when the moon comes between it and the earth, God is eclipsed by his son and recedes into to the background.

The belief that God in his justice could not forgive the sins of mankind unless Jesus was put to the Cross is one of the many anthropomorphic images that cloud our understanding of God. If we accept the traditional view that Jesus knowingly died in order to set man free, one can easily picture God as a despot who will release captives only after payment. Although St. Augustine flatly stated that there were many other ways in which God could rescue sinners apart from being induced by Christ's blood, the notion of vicarious suffering persists. Such images reinforce the doubts of the unwary and call God's existence into question. It must be admitted that the word 'God' means nothing to a very large section of contemporary mankind. In a world of increasing leisure and travel, urbanism, detached and functional relations between people, instantaneous information and perpetually available entertainment, God, when not totally absent, appears as an intruder.

Jesus, likewise, has become mythologized, by way of imaginative stories. Their visual quality lifts him above the earth into heavens where he sits at the right hand of God, remote from the world he inhabited. Because the words of Jesus chosen for the written records were selected by those who had no interest in biographical detail, there is not a single deed or saying of his that we can rely on as being absolutely authentic. Similarly, we have no exact record of his sayings, for he spoke in Aramaic, and our records are in Greek, and translations differ.

Historically we know nothing about the circumstances and the place of Jesus' birth. By contrast, what Matthew and Luke say in their account of this birth is 'gospel', not a report of facts but an evangelical reflection on the beginnings of the man Jesus. The first sure fact about Jesus is that he was baptized by John the Baptist in the Jordan River when he was about 30 years old. Although we know nothing about how Jesus came into contact with John or what impelled him to seek him out, his baptism was a 'disclosure experience' - a revelatory event or source experience that led him to believe that he was the promised deliverer of the Jewish people prophesized by Isaiah. The mystery of the developing consciousness of Jesus is beyond our understanding, but there is little doubt that he believed that the scriptures were a blue-print for his ministry. *'And he said unto them that all things must be fulfilled, which were written in the law of Moses, and in the prophets, and in the psalms, concerning me'* (Luke 24:44). Since Elijah (John the Baptist) was to precede the Messiah, Jesus, on *'hearing'* the message from heaven that he was God's *'beloved son'* was certain that he had been chosen by God to do *'His Father's' business.'*

This 'business' was the proclamation of the coming kingdom of God. What Jesus intends by it is a course of events where by God begins to govern or to act as king or Lord, an action, therefore, by which God manifests his being-God in the world of men. It is at the same time the final, eschatological state of affairs that brings to an end the evil in the world and initiates the new world in which God appears to full advantage: *'your kingdom come.'* Hence forward Jesus' life is given decisive shape by his expectation of the coming kingdom. It is what he lived for and it is what he died for.

There can be little doubt that Jesus' enthusiasm for the coming kingdom was heightened by the apocalyptic expectations of the period. For both Jew and Gentile, Jesus' time was full to bursting with an assortment of hopes culled from long centuries of promises and, more especially, of unfulfilled expectations. The world was conceived as a great hourglass whose sands were running out. There was the old age, which was running downhill and would soon come to an end, and the heavenly new age that would follow it when God's power would come visibly to light. This new age would either descend to earth, bringing a completely new order, or the righteous would *'arise'* to a heavenly realm. In both instances, the renewal of life was seen in terms of a super-terrestrial, heavenly mode of being. Mark's summary of Christ's preaching, *'And saying, the time is fulfilled, and the kingdom of God is at hand'* (Mark 1.15) assumes the imminence of the end time, and, by allusion, gave it to be understood that he himself would appear as the Son of Man to pass judgment upon God's people.

The scriptures sum up the prophetic vision of Jesus in these words: 'Repent. For the kingdom of God is at hand' (Matt.4.17). In other words, change your ways, otherwise you will bring about the downfall of your own world. Jesus' time must have been used to such prophecies, for shortly before hand John had similarly proclaimed: 'Repent, God's kingdom is at hand' (Matt 3.2). But in contradiction to John's fearsome predictions (threatening imminent and disastrous divine judgment), Jesus came with a message of salivation and mercy. For Jesus salvation meant exactly what it had for the Old Testament prophets: a human community of peace, where swords were beaten into ploughshares (Micah 4.1-5), and where the wolf, the lamb and the lion lived together in peace (Isa.61.1); because men did not rule over his fellows, but God lived in communion with everyone. Through the prophetic recollection of the accumulated suffering in human history, Jesus knew how human rule can pollute and enslave. In place of rule by power he sought a divine ordering, the rule of God, which frees men without alienation. 'You weep now, but then you will laugh.' (Luke 6:21).

But Jesus, like the prophets before him - who believed that God's rule was imminent, was mistaken. God's saving activity, the final eschatological state of affairs that would initiate the new world, did not appear. Believing that there was still some event that must take

47

place first, namely, that he, the messiah-to-be, must sacrifice himself as prophesized by Isaiah (Isaiah 53:1-2) as atonement for those that would follow him, he journeyed to Jerusalem to put himself in the hands of his enemies. From a political viewpoint, Jesus chose the worst possible time; from a messianic viewpoint, the best possible time.

When Jesus entered Jerusalem, hatred of the Romans was at an all time high. Having been free of Roman troops for thirty-seven years, the enduring military presence exacerbated the political situation. The high priests at the temple in Jerusalem were appointed by the Romans, and were corrupt. A rebellion in Galilee had only just been quelled with bloodshed and executions. People were talking about a new rebel leader, proclaimed by his followers as the messiah, and King of the Jews. Such was the explosive mix of zealotry and messianic fervor that the procurator of Judea, Pontius Pilate, faced with the possibility of political agitation in an occupied territory, left his administrative capital at Caesarea and went to Jerusalem to take personal control.

On entering Jerusalem Jesus was brought before the Jewish authorities for questioning:

'When day came, the assembly of the elders of the people, both chief priests and scribes, gathered

together, and they brought him to their council. They said, "If you are the Messiah, tell us." He replied, "If I tell you, you will not believe; and if I question you, you will not answer. But from now on the Son of Man will be seated at the right hand of the power of God." All of them asked, "Are you, then, the Son of God?" He said to them, "You say that I am." Then they said, "What further testimony do we need? We have heard it ourselves from his own lips!" (Luke 22:70).

By refusing to render an account of his mission to the Sanhedrim, on the grounds that only God can call him to account, he came under the judgment of Deut.17.12: If anyone presumes to disobey the officiating high priest, *'that man shall die.'* Because the death penalty was not an option for the Sanhedrin under Roman law, Jesus was brought before Pilate for sentencing on the grounds that his claim to be *'King'* was a challenge to Roman rule. Pilate asks Jesus if he was *'King of the Jews'*. His answer, *'You said it,'* permits Jesus to stand silent before his accusers as prescribed by prophecy (Isaiah 53:7). Although Pilate could find *'no fault'* with Jesus, he acceded to the wishes of the High Priest out of fear of sparking another revolution, and reluctantly sentenced Jesus to death for the crime of sedition.

In the closing stages of the great drama of redemption, it is the Old Testament that determined the narrative for Jesus' actions. On the way from the Upper

Room to the Mount of Olives he tells his disciples that he must lay down his life and that they will forsake him (as prophesized by Zechariah) 'I *will smite the Shepherd and the sheep shall be scattered abroad,*' and emphasizes that it is his Father who dictated the course of events, '*It pleased the lord to bruise him. He hath put him to grief*' (Isa. 53.10). At the trial before Caiphas he told his judges (in a composite quotation from the psalmist and Daniel) that the conditions of his entrance into glory were now being satisfied '*ye shall see the Son of Man sitting at the right hand of power and coming on the clouds of heaven.*' At Golgotha when, knowing that the Servant of God must make intercession for the transgressors (Isa. 53.12) he prayed '*Father, forgive them; for they know not what they do*'. And on the cross itself, when Jesus appeals to God to reverse his desperate situation by conferring his blessing, he quotes the opening words of Psalm 22, 'My *God, my God, why has thou forsaken me?*' and finally, when no answering voice is heard, '*Into thy hands I commend my spirit*' (Psalm 31.50).

Although both the day and the hour that Jesus died are unknown, it is almost certain that he was not placed in a tomb when he expired. The Romans did not bury executed prisoners but dumped them together in mass graves. There was no splendor and glory hovering over Jesus' burial, no offer of wine, or gifts of myrrh and aloes. After the most wretched and ignominious of deaths, he had the most miserable and wretched of burials. Rome and Palestine forgot the event soon afterwards. Only Tacitus and Pliny, Roman historians, had anything to say about a certain criminal Jesus who was executed by Pontius Pilate for his 'pernicious superstition.' The Jewish historian simply said that Jesus was executed for witchcraft.

In Marks gospel Jesus' execution put an end to the claim that Jesus brought about God's kingdom. On Good Friday world history continued its usual course as though nothing had happened, as in the case after the death of any human being. It is not surprising that Jesus' ignominious arrest and death put a severe strain on Jesus' message and his own claim of sonship. Mark 14:27 tells us that Jesus' disciples *'fell away,'* and by referring to Zech.13.7 ('I will strike the shepherd and the sheep will be scattered*)* infers that Jesus' death completely ruptures the bond between his followers. Disillusionment overtook them. 'We had hoped' (Luke 24.21). They had to wrestle with panic, doubt and suspicion. Later on the disciples feel their faltering to have been a failure of their faith - which led them to repent, and eventually to experience Jesus as a 'living' reality present in their midst. This overwhelming experience was so convincing that in less than five years the 'community of Christ' was already widespread in the Near East: the basic outlines of a world religion became clear after these few years and were above all put into practice, albeit often in broken human form. Human daydreams can do a great deal, but thy cannot explain the creation of so attractive a hoax in so short a time. From a historical point of view this is unparalleled.

Christian communities are grounded in the belief that the spirit of Jesus is at work in them: 'For where two or three are gathered together in my name, there am I in the midst of them' (Matthew 18:20). Such a mysterious force does not emanate from a dead man who was once a prophet; and although this might once have been the case, it will have been so only for a short while. In the long run these recollections fade, and in following generations they melt into the distance where colors blur - and finally they are only a subject for the investigation of historians. Human memory is short lived. Thus the question arises: must not something have happened to Jesus, something quite special. 'What we have seen with our own eyes, of that we bear witness,' the First Letter of John (1.4) says enthusiastically. The author did not know the historical Jesus, nor had he had a 'resurrection experience'. Nevertheless these Christians had the experience of Christ risen. For Christian believers, seeing and hearing evidently have a deeper significance than non-believers think possible.

Jesus' understanding of his death cannot be known directly, only by an indirect approach beginning from 'what the witnesses testify'. Jesus said very little about his death – nothing in public about its saving significance, something perhaps to the restricted circle of his disciples when death was very close. That does not imply an absence of saving intention, only that it became plain after Easter. To demand that the death of Jesus should have only the meaning he gave to it is to ignore the Holy Spirit. His death means not only what Jesus said it meant, but also what it was found to mean.

Nevertheless it is clear that the final days of his life are bound up with the Old Testament and its prophecies. As Luke writes in the episode on the road to Emmaus: *'And beginning at Moses and all the prophets, he expounded unto them in all the scriptures the things concerning himself'* (Luke 24.26) The supreme authority which Jesus assigned to the Old Testament is only partly explained by his desire to convince first-century Christians that everything he said and did was the fulfillment of prophecies in the Old Testament. Jesus grounded his personal claims and the validity of his teaching on the belief that the Jewish scriptures were a true revelation of his 'Father' and the incontrovertible expression of God's will for himself. *'For I have not spoken of myself; but the Father which sent me, he gave me a commandment, what I should say, and what I should speak'* (John 12:49).

Although the Old Testament facilitated Jesus'

understanding of himself, his actions and ministry were driven by a pronounced consciousness of his prophetic destiny grounded by his *'Abba'* experience. He clearly felt that God's spirit was at work in his actions and his preaching, and thus in his person. *'And he that sent me is with me: the Father hath not left me alone; for I do always those things that please him. I am never alone, the Father is always with me'* (John 8.29). No person and no prophet has ever made this claim. The gospels consistently maintain that Jesus bore witness to a *spirit* which they characterized as *agape* (love) to an extent never seen before. It was not something gleaned from his teaching, but rather through a growing certainty that something here was expressed, in and through his person, which was yet other than his person. It was this experience which led them to state the seemingly impossible: that Jesus was wholly and unequivocally man, but that God was wholly and unequivocally present in him as well. Consequently Christians call him, with unprecedented boldness, albeit in words which appeal more to the logic of religious language than to reason, *'the only-beloved, unique Son'*.

Jesus' death, for the Romans, was a common place event, carried out without fanfare by the authorities amidst the indifference of a city preoccupied with preparations for Passover. The matter might have ended there, in which case Jesus would be remembered, if remembered at all, as one of the many messianic pretenders that emerged during this period and whose execution was carried out without fanfare. What changed everything was the regrouping of the disciples and Paul's Damascus experience.

What happened to awaken in the disciples (who were in no way prepared for it), the conviction that Jesus had *'risen from the dead'* we will never know. Nowhere does the New Testament say that the resurrection is itself this event, and John makes very clear that an 'empty tomb', if there were one, could not be taken as proof of Jesus' continuing existence (even if the 'empty tomb' is a historical fact, theologically it could yield no proof of a resurrection; a 'vanished corpse' is not in itself a resurrection, and an actual bodily resurrection does not require as its outcome a vanished corpse). Still, the fact remains that some time after Jesus' death that those disciples 'of little faith' were courageously announcing that the crucified one was rescued from the dead by God, raised up and glorified, and could proclaim him as universal salvation, first for the Jews, and then for all people.

How did the disciples arrive at their belief that Jesus was alive, 'with God', and that his presence was actually in their midst? The most likely explanation for the post-paschal apparition stories is that the disciples retained a vivid sense of Jesus' continuing presence which led them to experience that Jesus was among them. They all of a sudden 'saw it. This seeing may have been the outcome of a lengthier process of maturation, one primary and important element of which was enough to make Peter take action and bring the disciples together again. The disciple's vision of Jesus after his death was experienced as a revelation within the disclosure experience became the matrix in which faith in Jesus as the risen one was brought to birth.

While the 'immanence' of Jesus was experienced as a realty by Peter and his companions, and given verbal embodiment later on in the 'appearances', there was no such linguistic ambiguity in the case of Paul's encounter with the risen Christ. Paul had not met Jesus during his earthly ministry. By definition, therefore, Paul could not have recognized Jesus on the same basis as those who had come with him to Jerusalem. When people have more to say than they can express rationally in words, symbolic evocation transcends the impotence of conceptual articulation. There is no such hesitation in Paul description of his encounter with Jesus: '*God was pleased to reveal his Son in me*' (Galatians 1:16), a remarkably mild (albeit explicit) description, of the most shattering experience of his life. In any event, the reality and the mental image fused to create an experience that convinced him that Jesus was alive '*raised from the dead and died no more.*' Paul was not mad, as Festus thought, when he heard about Paul's vision of the risen dead. But given Paul's neurotic temperament and the stress of persecuting Christians, we can be sure that the stress under which Paul was operating could have interfered with his rationality and heightened his susceptibility to anyone or anything associated with the focus of his emotion.

The fact that it was the risen and not the earthly Jesus of whom Paul first had personal experience brought with it the conviction that heaven was the sphere to which Jesus really belonged. For Paul, Jesus Christ was God's son, in the flesh and in spirit. Although Jesus had taken the form of an ordinary man, he was, in reality, a *'life giving spirit'* that was able to impart to others the spiritual life which he himself possessed. *'As in Adam all die, even so in Christ shall all be made alive'* (1Cor. 15.22). Before his conversion Paul thought it absurd to maintain that God had intervened to raise from the dead a false teacher whose blasphemous claim to be the Messiah was a deliberate subversion of the Law. But after his Damascus experience he accepted Jesus' resurrection, which he had previously contemptuously dismissed. Jesus, crucified under Pontius Pilate, had been raised from the dead, beyond the angelic world, to the holy of holies, and was *'set at the right hand of God.'* Christians now had an advocate in heaven who promised access to God and eternal life. Yet despite the writer's spiritual ingenuity and persuasion, one may easily gain the impression reading Paul's epistles that

Jesus' living presence is remote beyond the heavens, and that the world that Paul depicts is more like a cultic sanctuary than anything else.

Although Jesus did not claim be anything but human and denied possessing any authority in himself (John 12.44), he has become a victim to the distortion of Paul's revelations. In the thirty years between Christ death and Paul's beheading in 64 A.D. his vision of the resurrected Christ became the corner stone of Christian belief. Paul is the supreme mystagogue. His vision of the risen Christ is a captivating picture of heavenly power, ecstatic, and awe inspiring. Jesus is Lord of the universe, the prototype of all created being, ruling and sustaining the universe in his resurrection power, since by his death he has pacified the dissident powers on earth and in heaven. But in spite of Paul's apocalyptic vision and powerful language, the fact remains that God, who calls us out of nothing, who is being and Life itself needs no avatar to unite us with himself. *'There is no other save me; I am the Alpha and omega, the beginning and the end, the first and the last.'* Man and God need a third party as intermediary no more than do two lovers.

Paul's mystical Christ, ignores, what for Jesus, was the most all-engaging realty of his life: his *Abba* experience. In calling God *'Abba, father,'* Jesus was either a megalomaniac (which goes against the whole of his life and activity) or he actually experienced God as a person – that is, not as some indecipherable cosmic energy, but as a personal God mindful of humanity, who '*Is for us*' (Romans 8:31). Titus sums up this infusion of God's spirit in Jesus beautifully, '*There has appeared goodness and the God mindful of humanity*' (Tit. 3:4). If we ignore Jesus' *Abba* experience, his life can be seen as one more failure which takes its place in the growing series of executions of innocent people in our history of human suffering. His *Abba* experience, the source and ground of his living and dying, which did not falter even in the face of death, presents us with a fundamental question about God. Either God is, or God is an illusion, and ultimately a utopian vision of Jesus.

Although Jesus' resurrection is literally improbable but metaphorically attractive, his crucifixion is certainly probable and in all senses unattractive. But it is neither Jesus' crucifixion nor his resurrection which are the primary and fundamental experiential fact of Jesus' being, but his *Abba* experience. Either his experience of God was mistaken, or the divine ground was present in Jesus to an extent that he was able to name it, know it, and love it - in which case something of eternal significance did happen: the high union with God through love became actual in this mortal life. Believers can assert that Jesus gave the world its most significant and compelling notion of God as an existing reality. Unless Jesus was mad, which is contrary to all evidence, we are. Though not an isolated event, it appears that Jesus' human spirit was taken over completely by God's spirit (or, as John put it *'God was in him'*). While God's spirit reaches into every man, it seems reserved to the outer accident of circumstance and the inner accident of temperament, to know God as fully as Jesus did. But it is the truth of this claim that provokes the recognition that we can enter into some subject-to-subject relation with that which is the source of all being.

It is a mistake to think that Jesus' cry from the cross, *'Eloi, Eloi, lama sabachthani?'* ('My God, my God, why hast thou forsaken me?') was a cry of dereliction, of absolute abandonment and rejection. This interpretation would lead one to believe that in those last minutes before his death he must have realized that his mission, and his proclamation of the coming Kingdom of God was misguided, and more heart rendering still, that his belief in God was mistaken. However, quite apart from the uncertainty whether this quotation goes back to the historical Jesus, in Jewish spirituality the quotation of the beginning of a psalm was an evocation, a reminder of the whole psalm. Now the basic mood of Psalm 22 emerges from three verses in particular: *'For he hath not despised nor abhorred the affliction of the afflicted; neither hath he hid his face from him; but when he cried unto him'* (Ps 22.24); and *'All the ends of the world shall remember and turn unto the lord'* (Ps 22.27); and finally *'Before him shall bow all those who go down to the dust, and he who cannot keep himself alive'* (Ps 22.29). This psalm expresses the believer's conviction that in the dark night of faith, in situations where God's help cannot be experienced, man still holds fast to God's invisible hand. The Passion narrative breathes the spirituality of Psalm 22, contradicting any notion of rejection or abandonment.

Some theologians believe that Jesus' suffering and death was a tragic historical misunderstanding. It showed that what Jesus said and did was irrelevant. It neutralized the radicalism of Jesus' message, supported by action consistent with it – and that opens the door to a sheer alleluia Christianity. But the New Testament thinks differently. Jesus' proclamation of what he called the kingdom of God calls for a universal reconciliation in which all master-servant relationships disappear and all world ordinances which make this reconciliation impossible come under criticism, as does even the human heart. The kingdom of God is a reconciliation which abolishes all exclusiveness and precisely for that reason becomes universal, despite and even in the limitation of a particular finite situation. The recalcitrance of our history and the radicalism of Jesus' demand provoked an equally radical final solution as a counter-reaction: exclusion from the society which he put into question. Jesus' disciples recognized this only afterwards, in what was the Easter experience. Then it dawned upon them that what counts is neither success nor failure nor misfortune, but the will and the action to bring about universal reconciliation without any privileges and exclusiveness, even if this happens only for a short period of time which is in fact brought to a violent end, a flame which flares and dies, for just a few years, in a small corner of the world. In this 'useless' love the disciples came to see the true face of both man and God.

6

There never was a time when I was not,
Nor will there ever be a time when I will cease to be.
Gita, Verse 12

We can ask about God because an awareness of God is present in the question. This awareness of being grounded in God antedates all conscious experience. *'Know ye not that ye are the temple of God, and that the Spirit of God dwelleth in you?* I have quoted St. Paul, and clearly his experience of God was a reality which transcends ordinary experience. But Paul's experience is not unique. There exists in man a capacity for perceiving the divine that, in its immediacy, regards not the ever-passing state of this world but the mysterious reality, immanent and transcendent, that we call God.

Though God's spirit is given to all, there are many for whom it is not easily known or readily understood. There seems to be a notable anonymity to the gift of the spirit. Like the Johannine *pneuma*, it blows where it wills: you do not know from whence it comes from or where it is going. There is no fixed rule of antecedence and consequence, no necessity of simultaneity, no prescribed magnitude of change. Paul tells us that one has to grow in sensitivity to one's *'inner life'* to know God, and because development is not inevitable, so results vary. But apart from cases of self-deception or insincerity, nearly all of us, at some time or another, though one may not have experienced God in the manner of Paul, has felt the presence of a mysterious 'something' both in our lives and in the universe. One may not describe it. Indeed it seems that the austerity of silence is the only way in which we can bring out the inadequacy of our halting descriptions. But the apprehension is real: the sense that there is something bigger than ourselves which not only supports existence but is the active power within the universe. Christians call this inexpressible element God - the creator who precisely because he is God, throws no shadow over man's existence and can therefore be present even though he may appear to be absent.

No one will be surprised that science, precisely because it is geared to knowledge of this world, cannot yield knowledge of God. God is not a datum of human experience, for in this life we do not know God face to face. Between this world and God there is no relationship that can be verified, for verification can occur only between data, and there are no data on the divine itself. Similarly, there is no technique or method of obtaining from physics or chemistry or biology or any other science an answer to the question, 'Why is there something and not nothing?' You can explain things provisionally by saying that this is because that is. But what is that? As long as one stays within the limits of the physical world, you cannot get beyond the fact that something **'is.'** In trying to find the 'really real' or the actual cause of existence, we are driven from one level to another to a point where we cannot speak of levels any more, but must ask for that which is the ground of all levels, the source of all being.

It follows that when ever we ask what is ultimate in being and meaning we are driven to the question of God. If we grant that the universe is intelligible, there arises the question whether the universe could be intelligible without having an intelligent ground. Evolution occurs according to the laws of nature and a set of values that determine the strengths of forces like gravity and the speed of light. But why these laws, and why these values? To account for their existence there must be a supreme cause that in some sense contains within itself the all possible values that could ever arise in a finite world. And so there arises the question of God.

Again, everything in our universe is contingent. Events happen according to certain rules. There is no necessity why they should happen that way, but they do happen. Things do not exist in nature by necessity. Nothing *must be*, nor is there any sufficient reason why anything *should be*. All the objects in our sensible universe have been 'thrown' into being: they cannot account for their own existence. But can everything be contingent? For if things exist while having in themselves no reason for their existence, then the more normal thing would be that they should not exist in the first place. But because things do exist, we must ask 'Does there not necessarily exist a transcendent, self-existent reality which is the source of all being to account for the existence of everything that is contingent?' The universe calls for a transcendent cause: a non physical intelligence that gives to *being* the fullness and significance it lacks as long as the question of its existence is ignored.

Then there is the question of morality and goodness. No doubt we are moral beings, for we are forever praising X and blaming Y. No doubt we have a sense of obligation which is absolute, a sense of something which on every account I must do, or on no account I must do. But is morality peculiar to the human race? If it is, and goodness is to be found only in man, then basically the universe is amoral, and man's aspirations to be moral are doomed to failure. But if this were the case, how do we account for intelligent choice and purpose? Our conscience is no random attribute or inheritance from our evolutionary forebears, but a fact of man's mental constitution. To whom do we owe it? *'Which shew the work of the law written in their hearts, their conscience also bearing witness, and their*

66

thoughts the mean while accusing or else excusing one another' (Romans 2:15). So again there arises the question of God.

Another form of the question arises when we reflect on religious experience. Such experience takes many forms, and suffers many aberrations, but keeps recurring. Its many forms can be explained by the varieties of human culture, and its aberrations by the precariousness of human intelligence. But underneath the many forms and prior to the many aberrations, some have found that there exists a reality that transcends the reality of this world, and is worthy of their devotion.

The question of God, then, lies within man's horizon. It cannot be ignored. What God is – the answer to the question, *Quid sit Deus?* What is God? – we do not know. When Moses asked God's name he was not given a direct answer; only *'I am who I am'* (Ex. 3.14), that is, 'what I am will have to emerge in your own history', or 'my being is such that I shall always be present in every moment of becoming'. God is that which alone *is*, subsisting by virtue of his own power, the immanent and transcendent ground of all being.

Although God's reality is beyond our knowing, we express his reality as best we can. We give God a name, but there are many tongues, and so there are many names. We attribute divine attributes by analogy, but we cannot dissociate the analogies from their imperfections. To make God a cause is to relegate him to the past; to make him an end, is to postpone him to the future, to insist upon his immediacy is to involve him in the hearth and family, in the occupations of peace and war. While our resources are not equal to the task of describing God, and however much religious or irreligious answers differ, is the knowledge that it is the one and the same God to which all men refer whether they are more or less successful in conceiving him.

The sufferings, the sins, the crimes, the destructive power, the sustained blindness of two world wars and the fears of worse evils to come, have disenchanted many with religion. It appears ever less capable to enter meaningfully into people's lives, significantly to further good causes, effectively to help the weak, heal the hurt, and give hope to the disheartened. At the same time, God, when not totally absent, appears as an intruder. To fill the increasing vacuum, science proclaims that as the earth is just one of the planets, so man is just one of the brutes, that God is a projection from the psychological depths, and religion a facade for economic and social interests. But this is not an answer to the problem of man's suffering: moreover it is clear from human history that suffering and evil cannot be solved rationally or ethically, theoretically or practically, by man himself. For if man could collaborate successfully in the pursuit of the truth regarding human living, we would be able to overcome the meaningless elements that afflict our lives.

It is undeniable that human life includes particular experiences which are signs or glimpses of an ultimate total meaning of human life. All our negative experiences cannot brush aside the 'nonetheless' of the trust which prevents us from simply surrendering ourselves to total meaningless. *'Take heed, brethren, lest there be in any of you an evil heart of unbelief, in departing from the living God.'* The author of Hebrews is saying that if there is to be found a solution for our perplexities, it must be found not in the consciousness of men but in God's will. But can God's will be known by man? Paul said that his apostolic mandate did not *'come from men or through a man'* (Gal 1.1.) but directly from God, implying that knowledge of God lies within the horizon of man' knowing. More convincing his is *'Abba'* experience. All four gospels declare that this experience was the result of God making himself known directly in Jesus. In calling God *'Abba, Father,'* Jesus not only claimed the reality of God's presence, but totally transformed our understanding of eternal reality. The love that creates and sustains this seething universe of mass and energy, of chemical processes, of endlessly varied plant and animal life, of human intelligence and human love, has a personal center! God *'is living'* and *'is for us'*. The wholly other is at the same time the one who is wholly near!

Leading figures in other religions have had similar revelatory experiences which convinced them that they had been addressed by God. Muhammad, for example, was so overwhelmed by the sense of god on Mount Hira that he experienced the divine image as the innermost possession of his soul. He knew with an overwhelming simplicity that there can only be the one theistic reality, one source of all creation and one ultimate goal of all human striving. Since God is the cause of everything, anything which disrupts this unity (war, violence, conflict) is not merely a *cul-de-sac* for human progress, but a sin against God. Henceforth Muhammad's life and message became a working out of the consequences of his vision that every aspect of life is derived from the unity of the one God, Allah.

But can the same be said of the Buddha? A Buddhist might accept that both Jesus and Muhammad surrendered their hearts and minds to God. He might even concede that their lives were a spontaneous response to the divine will acting within them. But he may also hearken to the fact that Buddha was silent on the subject of God. He declined to commit himself about God because, so he maintained, metaphysics was irrelevant to religious life. The important thing was the intuition of God's presence within one and (in his case) the revelation that man's spirit has no commerce with material Reality. In a famous Pali text attributed to Sariputra, the great disciple of Buddha, Mahali asks the Buddha if such 'intuitions' or apprehension of God were real. The Buddha replied, 'They are real, those heavenly sounds, exciting longing in one's heart. They are not things of naught' (Dig.N.i.152).

Buddhism is in complete agreement with other theistic religions that there is a single transcendent cause to the universe, and that salvation means transcending all contingent existence and reaching that changeless state which man shares with God. Indian religion in practically all its forms claims that man in his essence is pure spirit – though he cannot realize himself as such because he is gripped in the benevolent bondage of matter. Exactly what this 'pure spirit' is cannot be described. Clearly it has nothing to do with our empirical self, which at best is the vesture of that mysterious and unknown 'self' whom most of us will never discover until we are dead. Contemplation is precisely the awareness that this 'I' is really 'not I'. The real 'I' is beyond observation and reflection and is incapable of comment upon itself. This accounts for what is usually described as the 'negativism' of early Buddhism which declines to speak about man's relationship with God. Simply put, the 'spirit' in man is beyond description. Of this state it can only be said that it is the final stopping of the process of becoming, that is to say, of human life, as we know it.

Although our religious saviors had no pretensions to divinity, or claimed to be anything but human, all have been given supernatural status. Cosmic reveries have become incarnate in the figures of legend. Muhammad has ceased to be merely the Prophet of Arabia, who performed no single miracle, and whose life was marred by numerous imperfections, was transfigured by an apotheosis to become the pre-existent center and animating principle of the created universe and Mediator of Divine grace. Jesus was canonized by his posthumous followers as the final revelation and Son of God. The Buddha hypostatized as a universal presence was exalted to *Devatideve* (the 'god above gods'). While this may demonstrate the futility of atheism, the fact remains that millions of Buddhists the world over offer their hearts and minds to Buddha in words which in theist religions would be directed to God He is 'the self-subsistent Lord, the All–Enlightened, Knower of the World, Teacher of Gods and Men, the Absolute.' Humanity, in dreaming large, turns its idols into the likeness of gods.

7

Socrates, when accused of heresy declared: 'I do believe that there are gods, and in a higher sense than that which my accusers believe in them.'
Plato

Nietzsche proclaimed that the death of God was 'a recent event.' This comment was added to the second edition of *Die fröhliche Wissenschaft* published in 1887, so that the word 'recent' is relative to that date. So what he clearly meant by God was the Christian God, and that faith in this God had become untenable. It was not the ability to believe that has ceased, nor has the sense of God somehow been forsaken, but belief in a God who looks down from heaven with Jesus seated beside him.

Although the Church has modified its stance on the virgin birth, miracles, the resurrection and a God surrounded by angels, it has remained fast to the idea that man has an immortal soul. This was and still is the last defense against science. But this last defense is not tenable either, for it presupposes a substance, the soul, put at one moment into a man's body and surrendered to God after death. While this might sound spiritually attractive, there is no scriptural evidence to suggest that there is any such implant let alone that it constitutes the immortal essence of a person. When this last defense is given up, science will have conquered all apologetic positions, freeing religion to accept the explanations of science, while working out strategies for dealing with secularist views about the nature of existence and human reality.

Einstein said that science without religion is lame, and that religion without science is blind. The implication being that science is purely descriptive: it gives us quantative measurements and relates a fact to its class, without raising the further question why things are as they are. Religion, on the other hand, while it attempts to discover the ideal possibilities of human life, closes its mind to a proper understanding of the world if it chooses to ignore the facts revealed by science. To overcome these limited perspectives he proposed that science accept the implications of a transcendent intelligence, and that religion give up those dogmas that find no point of contact in human experience. 'There is a spirit manifest in the laws of the universe, a spirit vastly superior to that of man.'

Einstein envisaged a 'cosmic religion' based on a religious sense arising from the 'experience of all things natural and spiritual as a meaningful unity.' The source of this unity is a transcendent reality, a 'cosmic power' beyond our imagination to conceive. It has much in common with the Hindu Brahman, or 'Infinite Ground of Being'. Because Brahman is the totality of empirical existences, the material world only exists, so to speak, as a dream within the mind of the dreamer (Brahman). Likewise, Einstein's 'cosmic power' is 'without voice'; an immutable coeval with the empirical universe. 'The lord of the beings travels in the wombs. Though unborn he is born in many ways.' Faith – that encounter with a 'Thou' – is non existent here. God, as Christians understand him, is lost and religion with him.

But if we want to say more about God than that he is the ultimate ground of all being, we cannot avoid using the term 'person' – that is, a someone, not a 'something': a conscious subject, and not just a power that produces effects. Einstein was right to criticize the idea of a personal God from whose care one hopes to benefit and whose punishment one fears, but he did not appreciate the symbolic importance of the 'personal' for a religious understanding of life. A personal God is one who is concerned with people and their lives and therefore closely related to, and active within, the world and the course of history. If the personal element is left out, God becomes an 'it', an Unmoving Absolute, ever aloof in its deadening silence. Although the supreme spirit in its essential aspects is the changeless noumenal reality, its representation in the form of a personal God seems to be the highest open to the logical mind.

Einstein's awareness of the 'grandeur of reason incarnate in existence' led him to believe that 'mind' is the ruling principle of existence itself. Nor was he alone. Max Plank said that 'mind is the matrix of all matter. This notion can be traced back to Aristotle, who described 'Nouse' as the 'form of forms' whose essence is pure energy. Einstein saw that besides the sphere of reality that science reveals through the complex symbols of mathematics there is also the sphere of a 'higher Unknown.' To quote Einstein again: 'Science must incorporate a metaphysical reality into theories of matter. We may take any particular causal series by itself and see that it is truly necessary; but the whole series can only come into being in order that the one Eternal Purpose might be realized in it.' Einstein did not say this for the sake of explaining how we can experience God, or how God can act in the world, but because it made more sense of the facts. Einstein did not succeed in the attempt to create a self-contained and rounded off theological system, for this was never his purpose. It should not surprise one that as soon as he undertakes to condense his surmises into propositions, and to mould their content in definite forms, he was unable to reconcile the demands of his religious feeling with the claims of his scientific thinking. Much more remarkable is the deep earnestness with which he labored to bridge the yawning gap between the conflicting claims of science and religion.

While believers can agree with Einstein that the universe is the product of an Eternal Mind, in whose consciousness all space and all time are comprehended, they would go further and say that this 'Intelligence' is immanent within us, although consciousness may not bear witness to this uninterrupted working in ourselves. While Einstein's physics goes no further than to acknowledge the existence of a creative ground from which the universe began, he shares the religious insight that reality cannot be found except in one single source:

All things come out of the one, and the one out of all things. (Heraclitus)

Though One, Brahman is the cause of the many. (Rig Veda)

All phenomena, link together in a mutually conditioning network. (Buddha)

When the Ten Thousand things are viewed in their Oneness, we return to the Origin and remain where we have always been. (Sen T'sen)

"Existent' is indivisible, for where is the second power, which should divide it?

But there cannot exist several "Existents," for in order to separate them, something would have to exist which was not existing, an assumption which neutralizes itself. Thus there exists only the eternal Unity." (Parmenides)

But indeed even if the One is more like a Principle, and the one is undivided, then the whole Universe will be undivided either in quantity or in form... You cannot have parts of the infinite and the infinite is indivisible. (Aristotle)

I am Alpha and Omega, the beginning and the ending, saith the Lord, which is, and which was, and which is to come. (Revelation 1:8)

Understanding the universe in terms of the metaphysics here put forward, namely the existence of a timeless Spiritual reality that grounds all contingent being, has a number of implications for science, religion and man.

8

Man knows that these nameable fragments must originate in a unifying Logos, but one for which human speech and reason can find no word.'
Hans Urs von Balthasar

SCIENCE finds no individual enjoyment in nature, no purpose in nature, and no creativity in nature. It finds merely rules of succession. It does not ask how the movement of matter originated, anymore than it inquires into the origin of matter itself. Modern science has torn apart what, in fact, was always linked together – matter and its endowment of force. This is a typical expression of that illusion by which we imagine ourselves able to know what something really is by 'taking a look.' Empirical knowledge, the results of observation and experiment, is merely the beginning. It divides the seamless coat – or, to change the metaphor, it examines the outside of things, but neglects the non-physical aspects that are not observable.

More than forty years ago Martin Heidegger acknowledged the justification of the West to favor science and technology and of study in depth and detail, but at the same time he pointed out the bewildering one-sidedness of this interest. By constantly splitting problems into specialized areas, science increasingly ignores the wider context which gives things their unity and their essential connections to the rest of the world. While some form of specialization is necessary in order to isolate the main features of a particular science from all the fluctuating complexity of its background, it results in an artificial and excessively sharp division between different disciplines and their wider context and meaning. These divisions result in a pervasive form of fragmentation which, over time, is taken to be the status quo

Nearly a thousand years ago the Jewish philosopher Maimonides pointed out that 'Scripture supports the theory that the spheres are not, as ignorant persons believe, inanimate masses like fire and earth, but are, as the philosophers assert, endowed with life, and serve the Lord, whom they mightily praise and glorify.' He quotes Psalm 19:

The heavens declare the glory of God; and the firmament sheweth his handywork.

Day unto day uttereth speech, and night unto night sheweth knowledge.

There is no speech nor language, where their voice is not heard.

Their line is gone out through all the earth, and their words to the end of the world...

And then he continues: 'It is an error to think that this is just a mere figure of speech; for the verbs to declare and to relate, when joined together, are, in Hebrew, only used of intellectual beings.' Maimonides is making the point that the material world, the world of rocks and trees, stars and planets, plants and animals, rather than being the neutral subject of scientific investigation, is nothing less than a mirror in which one can see 'reflected the face of God.' Science has become a limited abstraction from the infinite subtlety of creation. It can be extended, but it will always still be limited. And beyond these limits, there is always more to be known.

Science is a valuable purge of religion, cleansing it of illusions and superstition. But it will always need the fuller viewpoint of religion if it is to extend its horizon beyond the boundaries of individual disciplines and 'loosen' it's rigidly held assumptions which block creative intelligence. The most common form of this assumption is the idea that the world is constituted by a set of separately existent, indivisible and unchangeable elementary particles which are the fundamental building blocks of the universe. Though these have not yet been isolated there seems to be an unshakable conviction that either such particles, or some other kind yet to be discovered, will eventually make possible a complete and coherent explanation of everything.

The theory of relativity was the first significant indication in physics of the need to question the mechanistic order. It implied that no coherent concept of an independently existing particle was possible, neither one in which the particle would be an extended body, nor one in which it would be an extendable point. Ultimately the entire universe has to be understood as a single undivided whole, in which analysis into separately and independently existing parts has no fundamental status.

The historical world of becoming is incapable of being explained in purely physical terms. Creation reflects the activity of an underlying intelligence or 'mind' which has ideal being and free creativity. It is this fact that is brought out by the so-called 'proofs' for the existence of God. God is not the cause of things in an ordinary sense, as that would make him an event within the series of events. The cause of creation lies in a sense outside itself. God is prior to this world, the Absolute reality known only to himself, without whom the universe would fall back into non-being. It is impossible to say what God is in himself. It is more exact to speak of him by excluding everything. St. John of Damascus said that 'he is nothing of that which is…. above being itself.'

Nature is a whole with matter, life, mind and value as its constituents. Though all physical objects may ultimately be some form of energy and possess the same properties, their sensible qualities which are different, are not accounted for by pure mechanism. As science looks deeper into the world of matter, it draws closer to the insights of religion – abandoning a crude naturalism which holds that the world process, apparently blind, developed human beings who can embrace the universe through knowledge, and discern an abiding spirit at work within the temporal world.

RELIGION is yet to embrace the findings of science. God is Jesus' Father who lives in heaven, forgives our trespasses, and gives us our daily bread. While this description meets certain religious needs, it ignores the order of cosmic processes and the infinite series of events which give meaning and purpose to evolution. Unless God is conceived along the lines of a necessary ultimate ground for the universe, he is in danger of being apart from the world and merely a witness of it.

'Ours is a time of religious decay. The permanent validity of religion appears to be lost. The mass of people have either becomes superstitious or credulous or indifferent to religion; the youth are agnostic or skeptical, are in open conflict with established society and with the authority of the past; people are experimenting with eastern religions and technique of meditation. The majority of mankind is affected by the decay of the time.' Evidently a recent, very modern piece. Nevertheless it comes from the Annals of Tacitus, a Roman historian, and was written about two thousand years ago. History repeats itself.

Today especially, the reality of God seems to be mentioned only in the utterances of believers and theologians who delineate a crystal-clear line of demarcation between the natural and the supernatural. The principal signs of God's activity in the world are taken to be those otherwise inexplicable events, apparently contradicting all reasonable explanation and laws of nature. Correspondingly, all hope for full and complete communion with God lies only upon death, when one has become detached from the world as we know it. Such assertions can no longer be taken seriously as assertions, but look like fictions created by believers and theologians.

If increasing specialization prevents science from speaking of God, one would expect it to enable theology to speak of God all the more fully, but this is rarely the case. There is a scattering of new theological fragments, and questions are sometimes asked about the composition of the gospels, the infancy narratives and miracle stories, and the sayings attributed to Jesus. But there is little evidence of religions engagement with science, or overcoming the many differences of opposed views. From a layman's perspective, religion seems to be ever less capable of entering meaningfully into people's lives. Not all, but some, religion is pronounced illusory, not all but some moral precepts are rejected as ineffective and useless, and some truth and values, while they have a certain esoteric appeal, are dismissed as mere talk. Religion undoubtedly had its day, but is not that day over?

The long process of secularization has meant that religion, and especially the church, has suffered a functional loss. The 21st century came into being seemingly unnoticed by the Church which continues to live in its old world, not realizing that hers was a totally different world from the one in which many people now live. The cleavage between the Church and the world has thus given the impression that there are two different worlds – the world of past memory, the Church, and the world of the future, that of mankind living within an all-embracing rational sphere of understanding.

The confidence that men previously placed in the Church has been transferred to the sciences, technology, politics, welfare work and so on – all of them activities and institutions realized within a rational sphere of understanding. The traditional way of speaking about God thus became gradually more difficult. The psyche of the religious man is scientifically interpreted by depth-psychologists (whose interpretation of faith and religion is, at its own relative level, quite legitimate) adding to the ambiguity of the nature of faith and belief. As a result many people who have been brought up as Christians quietly leave the Church, while those who continue to believe experience great difficulty in speaking of and to God.

With respect to Christianity, it appears to have been progressively losing its hold on the intellectual allegiance of an ever-growing minority of educated western men and women. The notion that we must take the collection of Jewish and Christian texts we call the Bible as 'the word of God' as proclaimed by the First Vatican Council (1868-70) and are therefore supernaturally protected from error, ignores the complicated and heterogeneous composition of the Bible and the many statements that in any other literary work would be considered erroneous. The scriptures are products of history, containing elements of myth legend and floating tradition that exhibits a process of growth with many levels of development. They are human documents written by human hands. Conceptual expressions are tentative and provisional, not because there is no absolute, but because there is one. The greatest idolatry is the worship of the letter.

No movement, not even religion, should be nailed down to its foundation documents. If we regard the forms as final, we are rightly skeptical when they are shaken. We may not chose to replace the text itself, but the historical survival of the truth it embodies consists in a new appropriation, which of necessity, takes place again and again. Our times are different; our habits of thought, the mental background to which we relate our experience, are not the same as those of the classical commentators. If Christianity does not have the strength to accept that the Bible, though understood to be the word of God, is in human language (Hebrew, Aramaic, Greek) and in the literary, rhetorical, and poetic patterns of human expression, which can and must be interpreted by human understanding, there are many substitutes waiting in the wings to tempt man with the promise of credibility.

The Christian claim that Jesus is the only means of salvation is one of the many dogmas that invite the criticism of 'spiritual imperialism'. The appeal to Jesus' universal significance is suspect and ideological to those who do not share the Christian faith. The claims stem from our divinization of Jesus, a man with a past like everyone else. Jesus has become exclusively the object of worship: a kind of icon from which the features of the man have been erased. The critical and provocative aspects of his message and stimulus to action have been lost in the smoke of the incense of worship and the eulogies from the liturgical altar. Such one-sided divinization, i.e. an interpretation which points exclusively to Jesus' divine side, neutralizes the critical force of his prophetic message. Buddhists would like to

87

believe in Jesus, but cannot accept his divinity. Hindus deny that we have life only in relation to God's act of salvation in Christ, and Muslims reject the idolatrized worship of Jesus and Mary as divine beings. They find it impossible to accept that the Creator of the universe could dwell in a human being, or that a man could in any way be God. Truly the example of Jesus in relation to God is an example of Adam. He created him from dust and then said to him, "Be! And he was". (Qur'an 3:59). Any belief in some definable form of the absolute leads to an unyielding attitude in which basic assumptions are elevated to immutable truths. In the grip of this attitude, people find themselves compelled to fight to the death over different views, even those religions which proclaim love for all.

Sometimes we must abandon a particular belief in order to realize another whose value is greater still. It is the demand God made on Abraham when he called him to abandon 'other gods', and it is the demand Jesus delivered to his disciples, 'He that believeth in me, believeth not in men, but on him that sent me.' It was a summons that was and is largely ignored. Jesus was a man with a past like everyone else. He and the other religious seers differ from us only in that they were pioneer researchers in the realm of the spirit. It is not necessary to attribute divinity to their being for us to recognize that they are recipients of special graces and, at their heart, an ascent to a mission. Because such people are special, with a gift that comes, as it were, from without, their missions are disturbing to others, and they are generally ignored in their own time: as a rule their greatest effect is after their death. In any event, to focus on their mystical experience, their holiness, their suffering, is to run the risk of becoming preoccupied with their person rather than on the mystery which they have access to.

Finally, with regards to science, religion does not have to fight a rearguard action against ever more intrusive insights into the forces of evolution. Its spirituality can embrace the finding of science, seeing it as another means by which the infinite complexity of the natural world makes known the mystery of being. St. Augustine brought the sciences and religion into harmony by reducing the latter to the knowledge of God and the soul and then made the sciences the means by which to reach this goal. If this remains an ideal, it is worthy of effort. Perhaps that the age of Religion as opposed to the age of religions is only just beginning, and that religion may yet, in Marx's words, become 'the heart of a heartless world' and 'the spirit of a spiritless situation.'

MAN is not abandoned by science, but his spiritual nature is ignored. He is considered part of the hierarchy of nature, and a subordinate part of it. Although his body can be broken down like any other object, he is more than an assembly of atoms – he is also spirit. In his letter to the Ephesians Paul wrote: *'In whom also we have obtained an inheritance, being predestined according to the purpose of him who worketh all things after the counsel of his own will'*. Written shortly before his execution, Paul reaffirms that man's beginning and end lies not with the dust of the earth, but with that which has no beginning or end. The universe is created and sustained by the one supreme reality: and man is the highest expression of the universal spirit in the phenomenal world.

The 'oneness' of all things revealed by science, is evidence that man is not a unit unto himself. The world is in him, and he is in the world. His history stretching back to an indefinite period of time binds him with the past just as his freedom engages him with the future. The value of the causal argument lies in its demand that man's existence and kinship with the properties of the universe need a principle beyond itself to explain it. Accordingly, science has been driven to enter the world of metaphysics. The distinguishing marks of reality, matter, life, mind and personality, are accepted as steps in the progressive evolution of one and the same fundamental factor, whose pathway is the universe within us and around us. Religion goes one step further, and so far as explanations are at all possible, identifies God as the source of all being, truth, beauty and goodness.

Still, there are many for whom this world points no further than to the nearest horizon. They will listen to arguments for God's existence, but no more; they will acknowledge the presence of churches, but overlook their purpose; they will endorse religious art, music and poetry, but reject the faith that inspired their creation. On the other hand Christians maintain that God is *'within us'* and is capable of being known - otherwise we should not even know what is meant when we speak of God. *'Had I not known thee I should not have sought thee,'* said St. Augustine, and St. Thomas tells us that unless we already know, however obscurely and confusedly, what He is, we cannot know that he is.

Jung's sharp conclusion, that all men experience God's imminence without, perhaps, recognising it for what it is, leads us to talk about love. For what we call love is the nearest many of us ever get to identifying the *Spirit* within us. Although there are many disputed matters concerning religion, upon one matter there is substantial agreement, among people of all faiths, namely, that God underwrites human love. *'For love is of God; and every one that loveth is born of God, and knoweth God.'* (1 John 4:7). Even if God is not accepted intellectually, or known intentionally, love, that mysterious *'agape'* which gives meaning to our lives, is evidence of God's spirit within us. What we call love is not an engineered emotion or a miscellaneous affection, not a biological impulse or an imaginary evocation, but a gift of the Spirit. In this world most of us know the immediacy of love in our relations with friends and family, and only 'through a glass darkly' do we sense that it is deeper and more lasting than any existential realization of it. John tells us that love is *of the spirit* and *'endureth into everlasting life.'* It is part of our spiritual inheritance and cannot be lost. It is the one thing that nothing can undo, and which not even death can take from us. Love is the quintessence of man's being, and our link with the eternal.

If we remember the wonders achieved in the course of evolution, the hope is not unreasonable that we may attain what Christians call a 'Spiritual Community' – one which transcends individual conditions, beliefs, and expressions of faith. In some form or other it entails the acceptance of a divinely sponsored collaboration in the transmission and application of religious truths. Accordingly one might expect a transformation of being that would result in a higher collaboration of intellects through faith in God. Just as the organism attains the height of its complexity and versatility under the higher integration of animal consciousness, just as the psyche reaches the wealth and fullness of its apprehensions under the higher integration of human intelligence, so also would human excellence enjoy a vast expansion of its potentialities under the higher integration of the spirit. If we remember the wonders achieved in the course of human evolution, the hope is not unreasonable that we realize the full unfolding of all human capacities.

The incertitude about our ultimate destiny cannot be removed, but above this incertitude, there are moments in which we are paradoxically certain of the return to the eternal from which we come. The divinizing of the life of man is the dream of the great religions. It is the *mokṣa* of the Hindus, the *nirvāṇa* of the Buddhists, the kingdom of heaven for the Christians. It is for Plato the life of the untroubled perception of the pure idea. It is the realization of one's essential form, the restoration of one's integrity of being. While we know not what we shall be, we may guess that we are transformed by our closeness to God into the likeness of that which we behold. In Plato's phrase, we will be 'filled with reality.'

9

Look at the incredible savagery going on in our so-called civilized world: it all comes from human being and the spiritual condition they are in.
C.G. Jung

The last chapter raises the question: Why then, if God is love, and is 'shed abroad in our hearts' and 'worketh no ill to his neighbor,' is there such fear and disorder in the world?

Evil is not an incidental waywardness that provides the exception to prove the rule of goodness. Rather it is a rule. If it is not a necessary but only a statistical rule, it is no less a fact and, indeed a worse fact. The hidden and all too obvious suffering and social misery we see about us seems to cry out against the existence of God. Man's inhumanity to man is notorious in every age of history and in every nation of the world. It seems impossible to absolve God from the wickedness of his initial creation and continuing misconduct in the world. The argument was put by Epicurus more than 2000 years ago: 'Either God wishes to prevent evil and cannot, or He can and does not. If he wishes to and cannot He is impotent; if he can and does not wish to, He is perverse.'

Confronted with the problem of evil, it is natural to ask why God created beings free to act in the way they do. Clearly it is good that God has endowed man with freedom and responsibility. Clearly it is right to leave that freedom intact, and refrain from an interference that would reduce freedom to an illusion. If God did interfere in the affairs of man we would be mere puppets. It would make our responsibility for the world uncertain, and our efforts pointless. Without human freedom God would be the murderer in all homicides and the torturer in all torturing, which is absurd.

A similar answer must be given to the problem of suffering. Evolution appears to bring about beings with more and more capacity for enjoying higher values. The increasing complexity of organisms is a precondition for greater variety and intensity of experience. But this same condition also makes greater suffering possible. It could not be otherwise, since enjoyment and suffering presuppose the same quality: sensitivity. At the human level, the capacity for enjoyment involves sensitivity to bodily experience as well as to moral, intellectual, aesthetic, and religious values. But this same sensitivity can result in intensely painful experiences. The freedom and sensitivity that make possible the higher forms of enjoyment also make possible the higher forms of suffering. It is an unavoidable corollary.

In the autumn of 1492, Giovanni Pico della Mirando, the foremost philosopher of the Italian Renaissance, translated the creation story into modern terms, sketching out in advance in an almost prophetic way the future of Christianity in a secular world: God was pleased to create man as a being whose form is indefinite. He put him in the centre of the universe and said to him: 'We have not assigned you a particular place to dwell in, a particular appearance; we have not given you a special gift, O Adam, so that you can appropriate for yourself any dwelling place, any appearance, any gift that you desire, according to your own powers and your own views. As to the other creatures, their natures obey laws which we have prescribed for them and which mark out their limits. As for you, no impossible frontiers will bar your way, but you will determine your own nature in accordance with your own free will, to which I have entrusted your destiny. We have not created you celestial or terrestrial, mortal or immortal, you shall be your own free sculpture and poet of your own image, to give yourself freely in the form in which you desire to live.'

Giovanni's vision of man without God, or rather, his willingness to live according to his own dictates, has brought him nothing but grief. Human intelligence and human will have not liberated man from the shortcomings of his own nature either personally or in the social and political sphere. The humanist program of a total liberation of man by man, which repudiates religion and labors passionately to build the city of man with the hands of man, now threatens all humanity. This is not a criticism of science, technology or industrialization, but draws attention to our failure to reverse the priority of living over the knowledge needed to guide life, and over the good will needed to follow knowledge.

It is a supreme irony that science and technology, which for the last three hundred years, we have hailed as the cultural force which will finally deliver man from all those things that religion has failed to deliver us – hunger, poverty, tyranny, and war – at this time represent the greatest threat to our future. 'Knowledge is power,' said Francis Bacon. But our dominion over nature has led to the beginnings of the destruction of fundamental elements of life; unrestrained economic growth threatens our survival; control over genetic structures and their manipulation conjure up disturbing prospects for the future; and the nuclear arms spiral twists higher and higher above our heads and given that a strategy of deterrence makes sense only if one is determined to use weapons if need be, the fact is enough to make this strategy inhuman and ethically indefensible. Once one gives these means an absolute character they cease to contribute towards our freedom and become a threat. The sciences are no more objective than other forms of knowledge, and in the sphere of human values, decidedly impartial. The concept of right and wrong do not belong to the sphere of science; yet it is, on the study of the ideas centering round these concepts, that human action and happiness ultimately depend. Certainly science does not have any letters patent by which in a legitimate way it can lay claim to the dominant role which it in fact exercises in the West.

We live in a sensate culture, in which very many men, in so far as they acknowledge any hegemony of truth, give their allegiance not to a divine revelation, nor to a theology or a philosophy, but to 'intellectualism', which leads the human intellect into hubris by imagining that only it, the intellect, has access to the truth. It may justly be maintained that the acquisition of reason is the greatest achievement of humanity, but man is not and never will be a creature of reason alone. There are, besides the gifts of the head, also those of the heart, which always relate to the whole. What the heart hears are the great things that span our whole lives, the experiences which we do nothing to arrange but which we ourselves live by. Progress and development are ideals not lightly to be rejected, but they lose all meaning if man only arrives at his new state as a fragment of himself. Because of the relentless drift to violence, and the apparent absence of any brotherhood, it is science and technology themselves that now compel us to raise more urgently than ever the religious question – whether man, without God, is capable of realizing his own salvation. The irony is more biting when we see how the East is seizing hold of Western technology and science for its material prosperity, while the West is looking towards the east for its lost inwardness.

Yet as things are, in the aftermath of economic and political upheavals, amidst the fears of worst evils to come, the thesis of progress must be affirmed. For the very structure of man's being is dynamic. His knowing and willing rest on inquiry and every act of understanding not only raises further questions but also opens the way to further answers. But if the thesis of progress must be affirmed, it must be taken to imply, not only a contrast with the past, but that man will consent to the solution that God provides to meets the basic problems of human nature.

10

Love has no errors, for all errors are the want for love.
William Law

Nightly our TV screens reflect the bloodshed and suffering of people in many parts of the world. Since the end of the Second World War there have been over 250 major wars in which over 23 million people have been killed, tens of millions made homeless, and countless millions injured and bereaved. Tragedy and suffering are the scarlet thread that runs through our history. Nor does the future look any more secure from destitution and distress than the past. On an earth made small by a vast human population, by limited natural resources, by rapid and easy communications, by extraordinary powers of destruction, there may arise sooner or later the moment when the unstable equilibrium will seem threatened and the gamble of war will appear the lesser risk to some of the parties involved. If that should happen there is the likelihood that it will mean the end of human life on earth.

Past history compels one to concede the helplessness of tolerance of reason, and the impossibility of any one nation or super-state commanding the allegiance of all mankind. I am not saying that there should not be a United Nations or a World Government, but as Arnold Toynbee in his Study of History, mankind's moral resources are the limiting factor for its success.

Karl Popper in a paper entitled 'The History of Our Time' opposes two different accounts of what is wrong with the world. On the one hand there is the view expressed by Bertrand Russell to the effect that our intellectual development has outrun our moral development. According to Russell:

'We have become very clever, indeed too clever. We can make lots of wonderful gadgets, including television, high-speed rockets, and an atom bomb, or a thermonuclear bomb, if you prefer. But we have not been able to achieve that moral and political growth and maturity which alone could safely direct and control the uses to which we put our tremendous intellectual powers. This is why we now find ourselves in mortal danger. We are clever perhaps too clever, but we are also wicked; and the mixture of cleverness and wickedness lies at the root of our troubles.'

In contrast, Sir Karl Popper would argue that we are good, perhaps a little too good, but that we are also a little stupid; and it is this mixture of goodness and stupidity that lies at the root of our troubles. After avowing that he included himself among those he considered a little stupid, Popper put his point in the following terms:

'The main troubles of our time - and I don't doubt that we live in troubled times - are not due to our moral wickedness, but, on the contrary, to our often misguided moral enthusiasm: to our anxiety to better the world we live in. Our wars are fundamentally religious wars; they are the wars between competing theories of how to establish a better world. And our moral enthusiasm is often misguided, because we fail to realize that our moral principles, which are sure to be over-simple, are often difficult to apply to the complex human and political, situations to which we feel bound to apply them.'

One may agree with Bertrand Russell. One may agree with Karl Popper. Indeed, there is no difficulty in agreeing with them both, for the New Testament lists among the effects of sin both a darkening of the intellect and a weakening of the will.

A human being is part of the whole we call the universe, a part limited in time and space. We experience ourselves, our thoughts and feelings as something separate from the rest. This delusion is a kind of prison for us, restricting us to our personal desires and to affection for a few persons nearest to us. Our task, and on this all religions agree, is to widen our circle of compassion to embrace all living creatures and the whole of nature. We shall require a substantially new manner of thinking and feeling if humanity is to overcome the limited horizon that emphasizes the disparity among people, and ignores his infinite value. It will come as no surprise that neither humanism nor science is equal to the task of affecting a 'new manner of thinking and feeling.' The impotence of common sense and the inconsistency of reason suggest that only in a limited fashion can intelligence and reasonableness have any real bearing on the conduct of human affairs.

Carl Rogers tells us that, 'One of the most revolutionary concepts to grow out of our clinical experience is the growing recognition that the innermost core of man's nature, the deepest layer of his personality and nature is positive and moral.' The recognition of man's innate goodness might be a 'revolutionary concept' for Rogers, but not for religion. It has long been recognized by all religions that since God is the ground and source of man's being that man's basic nature is good, positive, and trustworthy. Moreover religion, although it appears at odds with modern culture, and in spite of its doctrinal issues, proposes the only realistic solution to man's problem of evil.

As Popper makes clear, the difficulty of meeting abundant evil with a more generous good is compounded by man's self-centeredness and lack of effective good will. Rationalists believe that man can control his aggressiveness by his own unaided ability: that man's shortcoming can be alleviated by a transformed humanism based solely on practical common sense. This wishful thinking rests on man's proud content to be just a man, and his tragedy is that, if he is to meet the problem of evil, to be just a man is what man cannot be. Overcoming human error is beyond the reach of science, of common sense, through obedience to ethical laws, or evolutionary claims of our common humanity. One may agree with Donne that:

'No man is an island, entire of it self; every man is a piece of the Continent, a part of the main... any man's death diminishes me, because I am involved in Mankind And therefore never send to know for whom the bell tolls; It tolls for thee.'

But Donne was under no illusion that recognition of our common ancestry is not sufficient to bring man to accept his responsibility for the welfare of his fellow human beings. Rather he affirmed that only inasmuch as man cooperates with God will he be willing to meet evil with good and love his enemies. For if men could collaborate successfully in the pursuit of truth that regards human living, there would be no problem and there would be no need of a solution.

The goal of human history as mapped out in the first

chapter of the Epistle to the Ephesians is to knit together in mutual love a fellowship of souls through common participation in God's love which is eternal and binding. Put bluntly, man's task is to expand the horizon of his love so that it effects a transformation in human relationships. This undertaking is impossible without God's help. Even then it will be accepted by some and rejected by others, because acceptance is no more than the base and beginning for further development.

Although this book touches on a number of subjects, they all, in one form or another, voice the short-sightedness of a purely empirical approach to understanding man's nature and the universe. Quite simply, such explanations leave man without a home. Lost in the wilderness of space, man seeks for a meaning to existence and finding none, is left to believe there is none:

The rising gale of scientific discovery has blown away the chaff of traditional religion, and in doing this it has done mankind a service; but it has blown so hard that it has blown away the grain with the husk; and this has been a disservice since neither science nor the ideologies have grain of their own to offer as a substitute. (Toynbee)

We are not all saints, and not everyone can claim that they have experienced the divine presence within them.

On the other hand there are many who feel that there is more to life than the matter-of-fact world in which we find ourselves. Even if one does not revolt at the very idea that man is to contemplate reality through the complex symbols of mathematics, the cumbrous technical terms of science, at least one has to admit that the world of pure science is very different from the world of feeling and emotions, of poetry and dance.

Christians believe that man's 'instinctive' feeling of 'something other' is pre-formed in man's essential nature. It is nothing less than the presence of God's spirit in man's spirit, yielding an anticipatory experience of perfect fulfillment. Paul expresses this in the symbol 'God being all in all.' Since our basic awareness of God comes to us not through our arguments or choices but primarily through God's gift of his love, it can be disowned, challenged, ignored. Accordingly, one is to expect that faith is precarious, and that even those who profess to know and embrace God's love can fail to bring forth its promises in their lives and in the human situations of which those lives are part.

Because science is emotionally and morally indifferent with regards to its subject, it has nothing to say about human fellowship, religion, faith, or how to create unity among social groups, races and peoples. It tells us about the formation of the galaxies and nebula, of suns and planetary systems, the emergence of elements and compounds, the slow ascent of living things and their ecosystems, and while science has succeeded in making religion a marginal factor in human affairs, it has not succeeded in inventing a vaccine or some other antidote against violence and suffering.

The last words of this book belong to the author of Proverbs: *'Where there is no vision, the people perish'* (Prov 29.18). Here is the voice of religion making its claim to be man's principle activity. The statement calls for an affirmation of man's spiritual nature, of God's existence, and the solution God provides for man's problem of evil. The strength of its claim lies in the fact that its foundation is that spiritual reality which is the true center of everything in the universe. The plain fact is that the world lies in pieces and pleads to be put together again; to be put together not as it stood before on the careless foundation of assumptions that happened to be unquestioned, but with full awareness of the range of possible answers.

About the author

Vernon Anley was educated in Australia and in England. After leaving university he worked for the Ministry of Overseas Development in the West Indies before resuming his academic career in Europe and the Far East. He has co-authored a number of academic books, written travel guides on the Hejaz and Yemen, radio scripts, and articles on linguistics and education. His novel, A Carnival of Lies, about the complex developments in Germany between 1939 and 1945, won the 2012 All Editor's Award for the best work of historical fiction.

Reviews

A Divided Universe contrasts the relative merits of science and religion, and concludes that both disciplines are necessary for a proper understanding of life. This book is a rare combination of depth and breadth. *A Divided Universe* is a book to be read by anyone interested in the human condition and the nature of existence.

La Source

A Divided Universe gives a detailed and sustained defence of religion as a rational enterprise concerned with establishing the truth of theological propositions. The author proposes a re-evaluation of science and religion in a way that would provide the basis for an answer to the question of being in relation to the totality of meaning to which ultimately all our statements must be related. This thought provoking book offers a convincing critique of science and theology, and how both can lead to a deeper understanding of existence.

Oliver Scott

This probing book is a work of exceptional importance.

John Falkiner

A Divided Universe offers a vision of the human condition grounded on an ultimate reality beyond the reach of science. In the process the author develops a metaphysics that eschews religious dogma and empiricism. This is an important book that opens a new chapter to the debate about the origin and meaning of life.

J.L. Moore

www.ingramcontent.com/pod-product-compliance
Lightning Source LLC
Chambersburg PA
CBHW070827250626
47170CB00006B/2237